BIG 'N BURLY BOX SET 2

BIG & BURLY

REINA TORRES

Copyright © 2023 by Reina Torres

All rights reserved.

No part of this book may be reproduced in any form or by any electronic or mechanical means, including information storage and retrieval systems, without written permission from the author, except for the use of brief quotations in a book review.

AI RESTRICTION: The author expressly prohibits any entity from using any part of this publication, including text and graphics, for purposes of training artificial intelligence (AI) technologies to generate text or graphics, including without limitation technologies that are capable of generating works in the same style or genre as this publication. The author reserves all rights to license uses of his work for generative AI training and development of machine learning language models.

The CONTENT of this book and its GRAPHICS are 100% Human Generated.

Cover Template by: Elle Christensen; Clover Book Designs

Logo Design by: Sweet 'n Spicy Designs

BOSSED BY THE DAD BOD

Doyle Crane is the man people look to for reassurance. He's a rock. The people who work for him. The people who live in town. His teenage daughter even laughs at his jokes... *once in a while*. He keeps himself busy, so he won't think about what he's missing. What's even worse is he's found her. New in town, making a new life for herself. What he wouldn't do to get his hands on her, but he's afraid he'll scare her away. She's just too sweet to be bossed around by the likes of him.

Shelby Akers is new in town and new to love, but that didn't stop her from falling for Doyle Crane the first day she met him. It wasn't love at first sight when he helped pull her car out of the mud or when he shook his head at how she was shivering in the rain, but it most certainly was when he took off his coat, wrapped it around her body and gave her a heated appraising look and muttered, "Someone needs to take care of you, Shelby."

Doyle knows he's too bossy to even think of getting close to Shelby. She needed a nice, easy-going guy who could be gentle with her, someone who wasn't him.

That all changed when her boss put her in danger.

He went from hands-off, seemingly unaffected Doyle to demanding, bossy-as-fu...dge, *hands-all-over* protector. Shelby couldn't be happier.

CLAIMED BY THE DAD BOD

She wanted to stand on her own two feet
   He knew she needed to be swept off them every once in a while

Everything Nathaniel Sterling had in his life he worked for. He had friends and employees who he cared about, but no one to come home to. He had a friend with benefits. No, scratch that. She wasn't all that friendly and lately the benefits… weren't all that great either.

Who would've guessed that he'd meet the love of his life over a box full of neon-bright condoms?

Evelyn Connors has had a string of bad luck since she moved away from Heaven, Oklahoma. Her latest job is for a horrible jerk of a boss, and she manages to white-knuckle her way through every shift. Who knew that a man would walk in one night and steal her breath with his kindness and the easy way they could talk to each other.

Eve had no idea that the spark she felt with Nathaniel would come back to burn her. The woman he came in with wasn't ready to let Nathaniel go and she didn't care who got in the way of her plan to claw him back.

Nathaniel knows who he wants. Eve.

He just needs to show her that forever can start with a moment, and he'll pull out all the stops to do it. Eve is going to find out that she's been claimed. And Nathaniel is playing for keeps.

WATCHED BY THE DAD BOD

WATCHED BY THE DAD BOD

Ronan and Poppy are next-door neighbors who can't help but watch each other when they think the other isn't looking. In this case, cupid isn't blind, but he's definitely got great aim.

Ronan Duncan has been a Private Investigator for years, and he's nearly burnt out. These days the only person he wants to watch is Poppy Tanner, the woman who owns the coffee shop in the next building. He finds himself scheduling his work around her schedule just to keep an eye on her.

Poppy Tanner is tired of being watched. She went on two abysmal dates and now Grant won't take no for an answer, calling and leaving her gifts that make his obsession crystal clear. He wants her or he'll make sure that no one else can have her.

One night, the motion sensor Ronan set up to keep her safe blares an alarm and before he knows what's going on, he's leaping across their balconies to her apartment to save her life.

Now he wants forever, but how will Poppy react to having

Ronan love and cherish her for the rest of their lives instead of being Watched by the Dad Bod?

CHAPTER ONE

The Milk & Honey Coffee Shop at the corner of Fifth & Cortland had only been open for three months, but it became his first stop in the morning a day after it opened.

The coffee was good. Really good. Dark, full-bodied roast, and even though the place was called 'Milk and Honey,' the woman behind the counter didn't push the sweet stuff on the customers.

She filled the cups.

And offered to top it off again if anyone stayed around to drink some of it in the mix-matched arrangement of second-hand chairs that took up the front of the shop.

Ronan Duncan was a man who watched people, learned their habits and their secrets.

No, he wasn't in some kind of government intelligence agency. There were too many rules and bosses that made him roll his eyes.

He was a private investigator who had worked for himself and only for himself for more than a decade. Almost a decade and a half if he really thought about it.

But even though he'd enjoyed the ability to choose his own work and clients, he was really getting tired of the kinds of cases that came his way.

There were only so many times you could investigate a business partner who was sleeping around with your client's wife. Or a business partner screwing around with the business.

Or worse, a spouse just screwing around.

Heartbreak sucked, but it was worse watching a person break down into pieces when you gave them proof of what they'd suspected.

They'd probably hoped beyond hope that they were wrong.

So, to see the proof that their spouse wasn't faithful? It cut deep.

Sometimes, it ripped right through the fabric of a person.

He hated seeing that.

Giving a person the evidence that they could use to screw over the cheat was worth the hours in his car or holed up in the lobby corner of a cheap and tawdry hotel.

A job well done for him, was getting answers for his client.

And yet, day after day, he was starting to realize he had questions of his own.

Was the job worth it?

How much longer could he continue to grind his soul into dust?

What did Poppy Tanner like to do outside of the coffee shop and her apartment?

Yeah, he wanted to know.

Because he knew what Poppy did at work. He'd seen her there over and over again.

And he knew what she did in her apartment.

Well, most of what she did.

The way their windows matched up over the tiniest alleyway between their buildings, he could see into her bedroom from his.

He'd never seen her naked, if that's what anyone would worry about. No, he wasn't that kind of a guy. He hadn't even intended to see her at first, either.

He just seemed to be aware of her whenever she was around.

Ronan could be fast asleep and feel her across the alley. He'd roll onto his side and watch as she walked from the top of her stairs and undress in front of the utility closet where her washer and dryer were placed in the same location as his were.

She'd get down to her underwear and then she'd disappear into the Master Bathroom, closing the door securely behind her.

It wasn't an intentional show, but one none-the-less.

Then, there were nights when he wasn't asleep.

Nights when he would sit up in his armchair and wait.

Wait for the lights in the coffee shop to go out.

Wait for the lights in the staircase to come on and then snuff out when she reached the second floor.

And when she'd strip off whatever colorful top she had on, revealing the color and type of bra she let cup her gorgeous tits, he might have...

Once or a thousand times...

Grip his dick like he wanted to strangle it.

And when she'd turn to shimmy out of her skirts or pants and wiggle that heart-shaped ass, he'd nearly go blind stroking himself over and over again.

"Excuse me? Mister Duncan?"

Fuuuck.

Snapping back to the present reality, he looked up at Poppy Tanner and her bright red lipstick, worried by her pearly white teeth. "You know you can call me, Ronan. Right?"

She gestured at his coffee cup with one hand and lifted the carafe with the other. "Would you like more coffee? It's bound to be cold by now, or at the very least, lukewarm."

Ronan, looked down into his cup and nodded. "That would be nice, thanks."

He held up the mug between them, waiting for her to take it from his hand.

"You looked a little lost in thought." Her words were soft and hesitant, as if she wasn't sure she should say them. "Whenever you plan to leave, just give me a heads up and I'll fill up your thermos."

He kept his gaze on her face because it wasn't often he got to actually look at her without a wall of glass between them.

Maybe that was why he didn't know that she wasn't going to take the cup from his hand.

He felt her warmth.

Her palm was under his hand, holding it and the cup steady while she poured a perfect stream of coffee into his cup.

The moment her hand moved away, he wanted to chase after it. Drop his cup if he had to, but he wanted to take hold of her hand.

Hold it in his.

Pull her into his lap.

Kiss that sweet, full-lip pout he could see on her face.

"You look like you have a question for me."

Her smile was just a tentative curve of her lips, but there was a dimple just to the right of those lips that he'd never seen before.

A dimple he wanted to see again.

Her gaze darted toward the door and he fought of the glowering look he wanted to give the man who'd walked in.

"Like I said, let me know when you want your thermos filled."

He let her walk away then because what else was he going to do?

Pull her back?

Toss her over his shoulder?

He could do all of those things, but there was no guarantee that Poppy would welcome them.

So there she went, making her way back behind the counter in time for the man to hem and hah over his lack of an order.

That's when Ronan got up, stretched his legs, and gave Poppy a slight wave of his hand.

There was an expression that crossed her features as she excused herself to fill his thermos from the large carafe behind the counter.

Ronan moved closer, his eyes fixed on her the whole time. He could see the soft flush of her cheeks, the rush of pink in the skin between and over the soft upper curves of her breasts.

And he saw the hitch in her breath as she looked up and saw him standing before her at the counter.

Poppy handed him the thermos and pushed her shoulders back as she met his much taller gaze. "Thank you again, Mister Duncan."

"Ronan." He raised a brow and set two twenties down on the counter, ignoring the shock and sudden reticence of her expression. "You don't need to pay me that much," she almost stumbled over her words, "you have more than enough on store credit."

Ronan liked the gap of time that fell between her words and his response.

With a slow lift of his mouth at one side, he tucked his thermos against his side and explained. "Then keep it for yourself, Sunshine. You work too hard as it is."

Her jaw dropped a little.

Not enough for just anyone to notice, but he knew her face. He knew the delicate changes that happened when she was lost in thought or working through a problem.

He even knew how to tell when something aroused her. He'd watched her read. He'd stroked himself to climax, watching her bite into her lip and shift in her chair.

And now, as she looked at him, her eyes widening, and her breath plunging deeper into her lungs, he knew that she was aware of him.

That, he decided, was enough for now.

After all, he wasn't looking forward to the hours and hours that he'd be huddled in his car, waiting for a chance to film his client's husband with his second, and sadly only legal family.

"Stay safe, Poppy."

"Um... You too, Mister Duncan."

– BIG 'N BURLY DUO 2 –

Poppy Turner was still floating over the ground when it was time to turn off the lights and lock up the coffee shop.

It had been a good day. It felt like she'd sold buckets and buckets of coffee. A good deal of tea, enough to almost empty a box of fancy teas that she'd taken a chance on ordering from Ceylon.

And then there were the baked goods.

There were only a few of the delicious things left at the end of the day.

A couple that she would eat because no one would want something that might be on the edge of stale.

And then two cookies, which she'd take over and lower the bag into the mail drop slot at the front door. Wrapping up the cookies, she'd tucked them away into a brown paper bag.

Someday soon she would get preprinted bags with the Milk & Honey logo on it, but for now she made do with plain paper from a local business wholesale warehouse.

She wouldn't wait until he returned. No, there was no reason to do that. There was every reason not to.

Just as she was about to open the front door to the shop, headlights swung across the windows and then pointed off down the narrow alleyway between the buildings.

Poppy looked at the antique clock hung at the back of the room and was surprised to see that it was barely nine o'clock.

Curiosity alone almost pushed her out of the door, but she'd seen Ronan Duncan come back early from work before.

She'd seen him glare at the cold night, the beautiful bricks that made up the walls in their buildings, and even worse than that, she'd seen him glare at the moon. Who did that?

Looking at the paper bag in her hand, she shook her head. No, she wasn't going to waste the cookies. They were her favorite recipe.

But she had to make sure that Ronan... That Mister Duncan didn't see her.

The last thing she'd want him to do would be to feign interest or force himself to warm up in a social situation just to keep the peace with her.

Oh, she didn't think he was a mean or a bad person, but she had the feeling that he didn't let his mask down often to the outside world.

She understood that in many ways, but she had a feeling that they dealt with it in different ways.

She was fairly sure that Ronan kept to himself, slamming doors shut on what could be a social nature, while she had tried the 'fake it 'til you make it' option. And she could put on 'the show' when it needed to happen, but she wasn't completely comfortable.

Before she lost her nerve, she opened the front door and darted across the open asphalt driveway. Luckily, the mail slot was just a couple of feet above the floor, so she let the bag hang from her fingertips as she lowered it into the opening.

It was the weight of the cookies that finally plucked the bag from her fingertips and the soft thump of sound made her almost regret delivering it the way she did.

Before she could chance that Ronan might see her, she darted back across the alley and closed her door behind her.

It was hard to imagine what it would have been like to be caught.

Would she have managed more than a few words?

Would he?

She almost stomped her foot.

At herself.

Because what kind of an idiot pines after the gorgeous man next door? The guy wholly out of her league.

A guy who tipped her way beyond the norm.

Smiling at that, she made her way upstairs and paused at the top of the stairs.

Distracted, she'd left the lights in the stairwell off and now, standing where she was in the shadows, she looked across the way and saw the light in his bathroom blink on.

She raised her gaze to the ceiling and told herself to turn around.

Told herself not to look.

Told herself it would be wrong.

But oh, there was that flame of curiosity in her.

She wasn't going to think about the exact location of that flame…

Poppy turned and stopped short.

Holy Hell.

It was like a dream.

A hot, steamy dream.

And she didn't want to wake up.

Standing in the doorway of his Master Bathroom, Ronan shrugged off his shirt, pulling the sleeves down his arms.

And oh, he was wearing an undershirt.

It's not like he knew that she had a thing for those.

The tight-fitting white cotton stretched over the body she'd only imagined up until that moment.

He was big.

Burly.

Built.

What were those song lyrics?

Brick house?

That's what she imagined if it were applied to a man.

All she could do was imagine what it would be like to walk up behind him, wrap her arms around his waist and lean her cheek against his back.

Ronan stood there, bracing his hands against the frame of the doorway, his head hanging in what looked like exhaustion.

Now she wished that she could have found the courage to knock on his door. Or ring the bell.

Would he let her touch him?

Smooth her hands over the rigid planes of his face?

Knead his muscles with her hands, like working dough for her pastries.

Images of a light dusting of sugar sprinkled across his skin dominated her thoughts.

She could almost taste the salty perfection of his skin on her tongue.

Squeezing her thighs together, she fisted her hands so she could keep her hands away from all the bits that were aching for a touch.

His touch.

The light slicing through her window brightened and she focused her gaze on his bedroom. He'd shifted and now he stepped further into the bathroom and the light from the incandescent bulb flared across his arms.

Oh. Dear. God.

He had tattoos all over his arms.

It wasn't that much of a shock. She'd seen the tattoos on his neck and peeking from his cuffs when he took his thermos from her. Or when he paid for his coffee.

She'd seen them, but it had only been a taste of the beauty under his shirt.

Now, she wanted to know what was under that tank top.

She wasn't a courageous person by nature, not when it came to men, but Poppy was quickly learning that her curiosity when it came to Ronan Duncan was quickly pushing her to the brink.

What brink? She didn't know.

But she knew that it might come to the point when she might forget what it was like to stand in the darkness and take a step into the light.

What would he think then?

Would Ronan find that kind of forward behavior attractive?

Movement across the way refocused her attention and she

nearly burst into flames as he gripped his tank-top and pulled it up and off of his body.

Her eyes and sweetly addled brain couldn't take in all of the skin she'd seen.

One more second.

She wanted to beg him to come back so she could have one more second to see him before he'd disappeared out of her sight.

Details might have escaped her, but Poppy Tanner knew one thing for sure.

She wanted him, even if it was just in her dreams.

As she moved toward her bed, she dropped her clothes in puddles of fabric at her feet until she fell into bed, her hands poor substitutes for his.

What else could she do?

CHAPTER TWO

A few days later, he found himself waiting at the door of Milk & Honey. It started to rain during the night, becoming an absolute torrent by the time he'd returned home, but even as tired as he was, he stood in the alcove with drops of rain soaking into his coat.

Ronan saw the wide-eyed surprise on her face and he barely resisted the urge to tell her that she needed to put a window in the door so she could see who was there before she opened it.

Instead, he looked down at her parted lips and struggled to hold himself back from kissing her.

She looked as good as her baked goods smelled.

Fucking delicious.

"Good Morning, Sunshine."

Her surprised expression turned to a quizzical glance. "You look like you might need a little sunshine, Mister Duncan."

Fuuuck.

Did her voice have to sound like whisky? Deep. Smoky. He wanted to taste it on her tongue and drink it down.

"Can you see that on my face?" He wondered.

Her eyes widened and then narrowed back to her normal gaze, but it was the smile on her lips that made him hard.

"It's there, but I think it's just because you don't have to hide it around me."

Her tone was soft... wistful?

He hid plenty around her. Like how much he wanted to step inside the shop, wrap his arms around her, and kick the damn door shut.

When had he become such a fucking Neanderthal?

"Okay, I'll bite," he smiled at her and breathed in, filling his lungs with her scent.

Her breath caught in her throat. Was she thinking of him putting his mouth on her?

"Tell me why you think I'm in need?"

He hadn't intended to put a double entendre in his question, but Poppy's reaction made him glad that he did.

Her fussy pink sweater only made her skin look even more rosy when she blushed.

Was she that pink everywhere?

Poppy exhaled and stepped back into the shop. "Come on in out of the rain."

It was a tight fit between the doorframe and Poppy's curvy figure, but he made it work, squeezing closer than necessary just to see how she would react.

If her shallow breaths and the little surreptitious lick of her lower lip were any indication, she might feel the same desire he did.

She lowered her gaze from his and turned toward the counter when he shrugged out of his coat, picking up her apron from a hook.

"I used to be a bartender." She reached for the insulated carafe she used to refill the cups of customers who used the chairs. And picked up two mugs in her other hand. "I liked getting to know people, but not so much the people they became when they drank in excess."

Ronan took the cups from her hands, the softest brush of her fingertips against his skin. "Were you safe where you were working?"

He saw the slight flare of amusement in her expression, but mostly in her eyes.

"We had bouncers, but my goal was to keep it from getting to the point that we needed someone to be escorted out of the bar."

"That sounds like a good idea." He picked up his filled cup and lifted it in a kind of salute. "Besides," he mused, "if the bouncers have to carry them out, I don't think they'd tip you very well."

Laughing, she sat in the chair across from him. "That's true. I didn't look at it that way-"

Ronan nodded at her. She wouldn't. Too sweet for a man like him. A man who had spent nearly every night watching her since she'd moved in.

"Besides, it's more fun when the customers at the bar are able to talk instead of falling face first in those horrible little bowls of nuts."

She shuddered and he lifted a brow at her reaction.

"Sorry," she explained, "those bowls are kind of gross."

He had to agree with that. "Too many fingers touching your food?"

She hid her smile behind her cup. "Exactly. I had to look away when they'd put the nuts in their mouth. I just... Oh-" Poppy ducked her head and mumbled under her breath. "I can't believe I just talked about nuts and mouths."

He didn't want to hide his laugh so he didn't, and was rewarded with her bright eyes and laughing smile.

"I didn't mean it to sound so... so dirty."

Her cheeks were aflame and he couldn't imagine a more beautiful woman, alive with laughter and so gorgeous she stole his breath.

Touching her would be the most amazing thing he'd ever experience, but would she agree with him?

Would she even want to try?

Attraction was one thing, but she glowed with light and he did most of his work in the dark.

"There you go again."

Her voice called to him, drawing him into her silken web. Not that he was making a lot of effort to hold back.

He looked right at her as he sipped his coffee. "How so?"

– BIG 'N BURLY DUO 2 –

"How so?"

Oh lord, what was she going to say now?

She shouldn't have opened her mouth, but he was just asking about the words that she'd carelessly spoken.

Why was she always getting herself into trouble?

If she was lucky, he'd leave, and maybe that would make this a little less awkward?

Less awkward than knowing she'd stared at him from the dark of her apartment?

Well, she better think of something quick.

Why not the truth?

"It's like your thoughts turn inward." Her lips turned down in a frown. "I know... I know I don't know you. Not really, but we are neighbors."

Inwardly, she cringed. What would make her say that?

"That we are."

He took a sip of his coffee and she tucked her legs up to the side of the big, oversized armchair she'd sat in.

How could anyone look so sexy drinking coffee?

Before she realized she was doing it, she'd licked her bottom lip while she'd stared.

He smiled and her brain went haywire. Was he smiling instead of laughing at her? Or was that smile there because he liked the thought that she was staring?

Before she could ask, his phone rang and when he reached into his pocket to retrieve it, she took a chance to stand up and move back toward the counter.

She wasn't about to listen in to his phone call.

Sure, she was curious, but she also didn't want to hear something she shouldn't.

Like if he had a girlfriend.

Or if he was... what? A... drug dealer? International spy?

Come to think of it, she didn't really know what he did. He came in and bought a big ol' thermos full of coffee for work. He could be one of those line-guys for the power company. Or a tech-guy who drove around to offices.

Or maybe a-

The rattle of his thermos on the counter top made her jump back and a soft gasp of air passed her parted lips.

"Sorry, Sunshine." He put a couple of bills on the counter, even more than he'd given her on previous visits. Before she could form an actual word, he shook his head. "Just take the money. I'm not sure how many people you'll get today with the storm."

She felt her cheeks heat up again and wondered what it was about this man that had her overheating like her old espresso machine.

"Well, thank you." She took the thermos and filled it as

much as she could before screwing on the cap. Then she found a sturdy to-go cup and filled that as well.

When she set it on the counter, he reached for it, but she held out her hand.

Poppy almost touched his hand by accident. Instead she left it hovering over his for a long moment before moving it away. "One more thing."

As she moved away, she mumbled an apology under her breath.

"You must think I'm crazy."

His laughter said he'd heard it.

"Oh my god."

"Were you trying to whisper that, too?"

She sighed and reached into the baked goods display, pulling out two muffins and placing them into individual bags. Poppy kept her gaze on the counter as she put the paper bags into a plastic container. "With the rain, you'd have mush before you got into your car. So I'm letting you borrow this container."

When she looked at him from the corner of her eye, he was watching her and the look? Well, it went a long way to warming the room around them, even with the storm outside it was overwhelming the heater she had on.

"Don't worry."

He smiled at her and the subtle shift of his lips moved his beard as well. It wasn't enough that she'd noticed it. Her body did too, and her thighs brushed against each other wondering what that beard might feel like against that sensitive skin.

When he spoke again, she almost fainted in mortification.

"I'll bring it back to you, safe and sound."

Holding onto her sanity by her fingernails, Poppy moved the trio of items toward his side of the counter. "Well, you stay safe out there."

Inside her chest, she heard her heart loud and clear.

'Stay safe because I don't know what I'd do if something happened to you.'

They were only neighbors, sure. But her crush was deeper than it should be. Her heart ached for him in some ways and her body... it ached for him in even more.

"Poppy?"

There was some serious magic in how he said her name.

"Hmm?" She had to keep her lips together before she ended up blurting out some ridiculous confession that would send him running away.

"You stay safe too."

Her jaw may have dropped open.

He said the words, but they were just something you said to people, right?

They were the same words you say to people you kind of know. The words you say to be friendly. Convivial.

He couldn't know that she said them because there were so many other words that she could say, but would never live down the shame of embarrassing herself in front of him.

And that's why, with her mind tied up in knots of shock and self-consciousness, she'd stood there, silent, and he'd let himself out and into the rain.

CHAPTER THREE

The rain slowed and almost came to a stop just after the lunch rush, which wasn't much of a rush. If it hadn't been for the four ladies who'd come in out of the rain and spent a good hour and a half chatting while they'd stuffed themselves with sweets and her herbal teas, Poppy's business day would have been abysmal.

Having the ladies laughing in the shop also kept her from mulling over her morning with Ronan.

Ronan Duncan.

Had there ever been a man so... manly?

Laughing at herself, she started to pack up the baked goods left in the glass case. It took a few minutes, given the amount of leftovers after the day, but she didn't feel too bad about it.

They wouldn't be wasted.

A quick look over at the antique clock on the wall told her that she would soon have some company.

Calvin Scott from the Mission Resource Center said he'd stop in on his way to start his overnight shift. She regularly gave some of her baked goods to the center if there was a slow day.

It was a little bit of magic, she reasoned, how easily she'd slipped into life in Center City. Chicago had been home for a few years and she'd moved there intending to stay forever. But the arts scene and culture weren't enough to keep her there when she had to look over her shoulder every time she stepped out of doors.

Leaving that behind had been an easy decision.

Finding a place to live with a storefront directly below had seemed like mana from heaven. Somehow, she'd just lucked into exactly what she needed to move on with her life.

Having a drop-dead gorgeous neighbor?

It was almost too much, but she was sure that what she was destined for was looking and not touching when it came to Ronan Duncan.

Tall, gorgeous, with red hair and a beard that she wanted to feel against her fingertips.

She was obsessing about him, but how could she not? Their apartments were close enough together that if both of their bedroom windows were open, she could lean out and kiss him.

Well, maybe.

Or maybe she'd fall and look really stupid.

Sigh.

She looked down at the box half-filled with pastries and reached for another scone to put in the box.

The front door swept open and she grimaced. She should have had the box filled by now.

"Sorry, Calvin." Poppy tried to pick up speed and finish packing. "I was daydreaming and-"

"I bet you missed me."

Poppy felt like her heart was trying to leap out of her chest.

No.

The knuckles on the hand that gripped the tongs turned white and the scone that she'd picked up fell to pieces in her crushing grip.

"Come on, Poppet. Don't tell me you're going to be rude after I've come all this way to see you?"

She couldn't move.

She was suddenly made of stone.

Where were those promises she'd made to herself?

When she said she'd scream and yell?

How could she just stand there like a stump?

And then she saw his hands, flattening on the counter.

Felt the cold that rushed over her as he blocked the waning light coming in from the windows.

"Look at me, Poppet. Give your man a smile. Make me feel like you're happy to see me."

His voice had started sugary sweet as if he was smiling while he said them, but by the time he stopped, his tone was sharp. Clipped like he'd sliced through them with shears.

"Poppet, I-"

The door swung open and a wave of rain speckled wind buffeted her.

"Oh, sorry, Poppy! Wind is really kicking up outside! I almost fell into the door!"

"Calvin! I'm glad you made it."

Poppy grabbed the boxes from the counter and rounded the counter, holding them out to the friendly face just inside the door.

She didn't say a word about her 'guest,' but Calvin must have felt something in the air.

He took the boxes from her, but he didn't make a move to leave.

Please, stay.

"Poppy?"

She lifted her gaze to Calvin's face and saw the hesitation in his eyes. "Yes?"

"Aren't you closed?" Calvin stepped toward the window beside the front door and pointed at the neon OPEN sign that was dark. "The sign says she's closed."

She struggled to breathe, but if she could, she would have sighed in relief.

"I'm an old friend. Right, Poppy?"

With her heart pounding in her chest, she couldn't give him much of an answer. She was afraid to say the wrong thing and set him off.

"You can leave us, sir."

That tone. That horribly superior tone that normally sent people walking away.

"I don't think so." Calvin didn't walk away. His height might not have been as imposing as Ronan, but he wasn't cowed like she was. Calvin pulled out a phone from his pocket and made no secret of dialing 911.

With his thumb hovering over the CONNECT button, Calvin tilted his head toward the door.

"I'm thinking you should leave, *sir*."

The air around her felt like a freezer, but Poppy did everything she could to hold stock still. She had no idea what to expect.

"I think you'll remember what happens when you disappoint me. Don't you, Poppet?"

She almost managed to swallow the lump in her throat. Almost.

But when the door slammed shut, rattling the glass in its frame, Poppy finally managed to gasp in a real breath.

– BIG 'N BURLY DUO 2 –

Camped out in the parking lot of yet another No-Tell MOTEL, Ronan waffled back and forth about leaving and waiting for another day to see if Tucker Greene was going to show up for a few hours of whatever he did in bed with his wife's best friend.

At first, Ronan had given the man too much credit, thinking that he'd use the downpour to shield his illicit affair with Laura. With pounding rain, he would have thought he was safe and Ronan hoped that he could quickly get the evidence that Tucker's wife was waiting for so she could file divorce papers.

At least that's what Ronan thought Tucker would do, but there'd been no sign of the man. He didn't use his car, but Ronan was on the lookout for shared riding vehicles entering and exiting the parking lot.

The only decent part of his day was the music playing through the speakers of his car and the subtle richness of Poppy's coffee blend.

She'd joked once or twice that he could save a great deal of money brewing his own at home, but he'd shaken off her suggestion with a shrug.

He couldn't tell her that he'd rather spend exorbitant amounts of money and see her instead of saving money on a home brew.

A coffee machine in his kitchen didn't lift his spirits.

It certainly didn't have her curves.

Or the bright light in her eyes when she saw him come through the door.

He could stare down the barrel of a gun and hardly break a sweat.

He'd dragged himself into an emergency every once in a while with a piece of his flesh carved out.

But Ronan was weak when it came to Poppy.

She'd been in his life for just a few months, moments here and there, but he couldn't see how he could stand losing her.

Even if it was just across the narrow driveway between their two buildings.

BZZZ

FLASH

BZZZZZZ

FLASH

Setting down his camera and telescopic lens, Ronan picked up his phone and turned it over.

The alerts on his phone twisted in his gut like a knife.

911 CALLED TO MILK & HONEY

"What the fu-"

Another buzz and flash heralded a second alert.

SECURITY VIDEO ALERT

Ronan nearly dropped his phone as he tried to open the EYE SECURITY APP. "Fucking butterfingers."

Luckily for his sanity, it opened a moment later.

The video footage made his heart pound and his blood pressure rise dangerously in his veins.

A man in a suit walked into Poppy's place and stopped on the other side of the counter from her.

He had no way of hearing him speak since the cameras he had on her store were outside in the elements.

Ronan knew he'd change that, because as the man stood there, Poppy didn't look up.

She didn't smile.

She didn't even move.

It was totally unlike her.

He didn't know how he knew it, but he bet she was terrified.

When the door opened again, the edges of his vision darkened with anger.

What now?

Poppy lurched away from the counter and straight to the man at the door.

Ronan fought down the wave of jealousy that tried to choke the air from his lungs. As soon as the man took hold of the boxes, he turned his head and Ronan saw his face.

Calvin. Calvin Scott. He worked at the Mission where Poppy donates baked goods from her shop.

Sitting up in his seat, he clipped his cellphone to a holder on the dashboard and put on his seatbelt.

He watched as Calvin stayed by Poppy's side as the other man walked out.

Flicking on his wipers, Ronan grumbled under his breath. With the distortion from the rain on the window glass, he doubted that he'd get a really good image of the man's face, but he had friends with some serious graphic skills.

There had to be a vehicle nearby.

He had a bottle of Scotch for his friend in the Center City Police Department who could help him with identifying the license plate.

No matter what he would have to do, he'd do it.

Because he was going to find the man in the suit and make it excruciatingly clear that Poppy wasn't someone he should approach.

If this man wanted to scare her? He'd find himself in a world of hurt.

There just wasn't a place in Poppy's life for people who wanted to hurt her.

He was on the road, forcing his attention onto the world around him. Ronan wanted to watch the video again and see what kinds of mannerisms he could pick up since he had a back view and maybe a side view angle on another camera.

He'd pour over the footage when he was home.

But only after he'd seen to Poppy's safety and comfort.

He spared a momentary glance at the video feed and saw Calvin sitting her down in a chair, his hand squeezing hers.

Yeah. Ronan knew he needed to calm down.

Instinct wanted to rip Calvin's hand from hers, but he'd take a knife to the gut before he acted like a knuckle-dragging idiot.

Poppy's normal posture gave her the air of royalty, but in her chair, she was crouched over, curling into herself.

The last thing he'd do was make her even more worried or self-conscious. He was going to help her, not hurt her.

Tucker Greene's wife would get her proof of his bad behavior. He'd make sure of it, but at the moment, Ronan had a sinking feeling that Poppy's unwanted visitor had come to cause trouble.

Ronan was going to do whatever it took to stop him.

CHAPTER FOUR

Her home was her castle.

If she said it out loud, surely someone would roll their eyes or give her a 'look.'

But it was the truth.

Her little apartment had some problems but she had her space. She could curl up on her thrifted couch, pull one of her grandmother's crazy quilts up around her shoulders and up to her neck and settle in.

She could close the door and shut everyone out.

That's exactly why she chose to speak to the police in her coffee shop.

The officers had separated her from Calvin and she understood the reason.

They both had to give their statement and the officers were doing their jobs. Independent statements.

Independent interaction with the officers.

She'd been through it before.

Numerous times.

It was how she got her restraining order against...

She closed her eyes, squeezing them tight to shut out the odd bustle of activity in the room.

She had a number of officers who came in to get coffee, but these officers were there for another reason entirely.

Because her sanctuary had been ripped apart.

How had he found her?

"Poppy?"

His voice sounded like a dream and she wrapped her arms around herself to hold tight to it before it was ripped away from her too.

"Sir? Sir, stop! This is an active crime s- Sir! You can't go-"

"Poppy? Shit."

Her eyes opened wide and her gaze fixed on Ronan as he pushed past the officer who had been standing in the doorway.

"Are you okay?"

She watched him move past the other officers. The men in uniform didn't put up much of a fuss as he shouldered through.

Poppy's mind struggled with the question as he moved closer and closer.

"Are you hurt?"

She felt him take her hand and all she could do was hold on to it as she dropped her gaze to see the way his larger hand almost swallowed her own.

"Hey, did someone think to call an ambulance to check her for shock?"

A nearby officer, someone just behind her shoulder, spoke. "We offered to call a bus, Sir. She declined."

Poppy heard Ronan's frustrated huff of breath and that grumble brought her around. It made her smile.

"Mister Duncan?" It soothed her to say the words.

"Ronan."

He said it so forcefully that one of the officers swore under his breath.

"Sorry," his apology sounded like it hurt. Another exhale, this time, slower and he was able to speak in a softer tone. "I'm struggling a little, Poppy."

Struggling?

Ronan Duncan?

She'd come to see him like some mythical warrior. Like Connor MacLeod. Or William Wallace. They deserved both names to be spoken with reverence.

She kept her gaze locked onto his face, because she finally had an excuse to look her fill at him.

His face was different. The planes and lines of his stunningly gorgeous face were tighter, drawn. And in his eyes, she saw what she could only describe as a searching look.

What could a man like him be looking for in a girl like her?

If it was in her power to give him, she most certainly would.

As she looked into his eyes, the shadows around them eased and the tight line of his lips softened until she could see some of the color returning to them.

She felt a smile touch her lips as she realized the transformation that had come over his features.

"There," she spoke softly to him, "I was beginning to worry about you."

His eyes widened at that. "You were worrying about me?"

"Of course." She almost winced at her own matter-of-fact tone. "You look like you're hurting."

He leaned closer and suddenly she felt like she was sharing space with him.

"Baby, I came here to check on you."

"On me?" She shook her head. "Maybe I do need that ambulance. I must have hit my head."

The instant she said that, she was sure that she'd fallen into a rabbit hole.

"How did you even know something happened?"

The same officer who'd been shouldered aside by Ronan, stepped forward and into her line of sight. "Miss? If you're okay with this... gentleman here. We've got your statement and that of the other gentleman. We can put things in motion at the station." He looked down at his notepad. "And we'll contact the Chicago Police about the restraining order violation."

Poppy felt Ronan tremble through their joined hands and the energy she felt rushing over her was like a volcano with pressure building, welling up inside.

She looked at the officer and mustered up as much of a smile as she could. "Thank you. Really, thanks."

The officers looked at each other before filing out of the door. The last officer paused with his hand on the doorknob, and when she gave him a little nod, his lips compressed into a thin line before he set the internal lock and closed the door behind him.

They were alone.

The door locked and the world, in effect, shut out.

Poppy let out a breath, and at the end, her shoulders shook.

Before she realized what was happening, Poppy felt a wide, warm hand on her back, drawing her forward.

She didn't worry about tipping forward and off her chair. Poppy felt his solid and steadying presence, comforted by every inch where they touched.

He drew her closer until her forehead touched his shoulder.

She felt him groan as his hand settled on her lower back.

"Why are you shaking?" He didn't move or speak, but he didn't pull away either. It made her bolder. "Did you hear what happened?"

– BIG 'N BURLY DUO 2 –

"Did you hear what happened?"

He wanted to shout down the heavens, but he didn't want to scare her. That's the last thing he wanted to do.

"I heard it. I saw it. And I swear on everything I hold dear that I'm going to do what it takes to stop him from coming anywhere near you, ever again."

As hard as it was to breathe, he had to, so he forced himself to fill his lungs and let it back out again, calming his nerves as well.

After several breaths, he realized that she was breathing with him.

And her hand? Poppy's soft and supple hand was stroking his.

"Do you know what you do to me?"

She stilled and slowly lifted her head.

Her eyes, when they met his, were wide and full of her innocence. "Me?"

"You." Ronan drew their joined hands up and held her hand against his heart. "It killed me to see you afraid."

Her chin dropped slightly and her tongue swept over her lower lip. He knew this pensive mood. Sometimes when she was pondering over a choice she had to make, she'd do much of the same gesture.

"You could tell I was afraid?"

"I can tell a lot of things about you, just by looking at you."

She almost laughed in surprise. Poppy looked positively stunned by his words. "I guess that makes sense," she shrugged. "I'm not all that complicated."

"You say that," he reasoned, "as if it's a bad thing. I think it's part of your beauty. We live in a world where so many people think it's a badge of honor to hide their feelings behind a pretty mask. I don't want to worry that I'm being lied to and I think you wear your heart on your sleeve. That's a beautiful thing, Poppy."

"And you?" She tilted her head to the side as she regarded him. "I have no idea about you. I'm still trying to wrap my mind around how you saw what was happening? Are you trying to tell me you're some kind of psychic?"

"No." He shook his head and sighed. "I'm not psychic, Poppy, but I do have security cameras on my building and I know that you don't have any on yours. I have a few pointed toward your shop. I wanted to know that you were protected.

"Now I know I didn't do enough."

He felt her still against him, and he only wanted to bring her closer.

"I need you to tell me who this guy is, Poppy. I need to know so I can stop him from getting anywhere near you."

She shook her head and leaned back, pulling away. "You shouldn't get involved in this, Ronan. It's not worth it."

"First," his voice was rough to his own ears, "I'm already involved, Poppy. If it's a danger to you, I'm involved. And don't ever say you're not worth it. You are worth it and I'm going to keep telling you that until you believe it."

He could tell that she was trying not to believe his words, but he'd deal with that, too. He'd get through to her no matter what it took.

"What about second?"

Her voice was soft, but there was a light tone of inquiry in it, and a spark of humor in her eyes.

That made him smile to see it.

"Second, what?"

She huffed a little, but at last she explained. "I want to know what you were going to say to me next."

"Second," he repeated, "I think you were a little afraid of me, but you're not anymore. I can work with that."

Poppy shook her head and leaned back to look at him. "Afraid of you? But... if I was, how do you know that I'm not anymore? You can't know me that well."

"I know you, Poppy. So much so that I know until today, until just a few moments ago, you always called me Mister Duncan. You put that space between us because you weren't sure that you could trust me.

"Today, you called me Ronan. That made all the difference to me."

"Oh?" He heard a little sass in her voice and saw the lift of her cheeks as her eyes fixed on his face. "What difference is that?"

He was going to tell her, but he was also going to show her.

Lifting her with hardly any effort at all, he settled her in his lap and tipped her chin up with the crook of his finger. "The difference is that you see me as a man and not just a customer that comes here to buy my coffee or your neighbor across the drive. And unless you tell me no, I'm going to kiss you, Poppy Tanner, so you know that I see you as a woman."

"You're going to... to kiss me?"

"Unless you say no."

He watched her swallow, and his eyes followed the distraction of the delicate length of her throat.

When he lifted his gaze to meet her eyes again, she smiled. "Well, I'm saying yes."

Thank fuck.

Ronan leaned in and kissed her.

CHAPTER FIVE

Oh. God. I'm kissing Ronan Duncan.

He had his hands on her. One on her hip. One on her cheek.

And her hands? She couldn't quite decide what to do with them. His shoulders. His upper arms. His forearms. It was like she was discovering every inch of his arms by touch alone.

It didn't help that his lips were like a drug.

They made her dreamy and floaty.

And when she leaned into his kiss, she leaned against something else.

Poppy's breath caught in her lungs and she tensed on his lap.

"Should I apologize?"

She almost stumbled off his lap, her heels wobbling on the worn wooden floor.

Ronan reached out a hand and steadied her, sending a shiver up from her hand where he touched her. "Are you okay?"

She nodded before she could think about an answer, her

free hand pressing over her heart. "I think my heart is running a marathon right now and I'm not built for marathons."

She waited for Ronan to laugh at her usual self-deprecating humor, but he didn't, keeping his gaze on her face.

When he opened his mouth to speak, she saw the tip of his tongue trace along the inside of his lower lip.

That tongue had just been in her mouth, sweeping against her own. The heavy pull of desire pooled between her legs, and her nipples tingled with need.

"I could think of a few marathon activities I'd like to do with you, Poppy."

Her mind filled with hazy, heated images and her knees went weak.

"Hey," he drew her back onto his lap, "this isn't the time for that discussion, sweetheart. I need you to give me a name."

"A name?" She shook her head, struggling to climb out of the haze of desire that was still pulsing in her veins. "Who?"

"The man who came here tonight, Poppy. Tell me who it is so I can keep him the fuck away from you."

She smiled, but it wasn't because she was happy. It was the same smile she had when she was nervous, on the verge of panic.

"I don't want to talk about it."

The look on his face was something she'd never seen before.

He looked at her and she felt... seen.

"We need to talk about it, Poppy. I don't like thinking that you're in danger, but I could see it in your body, your posture. You were afraid and he was the reason. Tell me who he is and I can help."

She couldn't help but fidget. "The police know. I gave them the information."

He took her hands in his. "The number of officers assigned

to our area of the city on any given shift are already spread thin. I've never told you what I do, not exactly."

Poppy nodded. "I think you said you do research for folks." His smile was addictive.

"I'm a private investigator."

She felt her nose wrinkle up a bit in confusion. "People really do that? I haven't seen much about that on TV that isn't in black and white."

"What about Magnum P.I.?"

She shook her head and smiled. "Okay, that was in color, but this is a long way from Hawaii."

"The job description isn't super sexy. Stakeouts can get boring and monotonous, but we can help. *I*," he put emphasis on his words, "can help people." He brought her hands up to his mouth and kissed the backs of her hands. "I don't take a case where the client isn't deserving. I only work for people who need the help, not the people that hurt others. Someone hurt you, someone scared you, and I'm not going to let that go."

"Why?"

The question was out before she was even aware that she wanted to know.

"I mean, he's not the kind of guy that you go up against, Ronan. He's powerful. He's not a guy that understands the word no when he wants something and-"

"Did he hurt you?" Ronan's hold on her hands tightened, but it didn't hurt at all. She could feel him shake, but he was still remarkably gentle with her. "Did he-"

"We went on a few dates, but there was something about him. He felt off." She shivered and then steeled herself to get through the retelling. "At first he just kept calling me or sending me flowers. I guess he thought that would be enough, but there was something inside me." She put her hand against her middle and swallowed hard. "It told me to keep turning him down. He started sending me other presents. Dead flowers. Those I tried to laugh off.

"Then other things started to show up on my doorstep. Dead animals. Pictures of me in all sorts of places. Pictures of me walking to work. Pictures of me shopping in stores. Pictures of me...changing clothes with little typewritten notes.

ARE YOU WEARING THAT FOR ME?

CAN'T WAIT TO TAKE THAT OFF OF YOU

MAYBE IT'S TIME THAT I TIE YOU UP

That's when I called the police. It took me talking to a handful of police officers before someone took it seriously. And even then, trying to get a court order to make him stay away felt like I was even more in his power. He'd come to court. He'd stare at me, smiling like he was possessed or something, but I had an officer who believed in me, and we got that TRO."

"Temporary restraining order." Ronan's voice sounded strained.

"Yeah, but I'm sure you know about those being a private investigator."

"I know about them, but those are clients who had to get one for their safety, Poppy. You're not a client."

She wanted to ask about what he meant, but she just sat there looking at him, drinking in the sight of this deliciously hot man looking at her as if she meant everything to him.

The last thing she wanted to do was burst that bubble.

"Give me a name, Poppy. Give me his name because I'm going to do whatever it takes to keep you safe."

"Why?" She wished she could reach out and snatch the question from the air and swallow it back down.

A smile warmed his lips.

"Why, Poppy? Because you deserve to be happy. You

deserve to be safe. And when I can make sure that you're not afraid anymore, I'm going to ask you to be mine."

"What?" She shook her head and looked away as her mind tried to work through the words that she'd heard. "You want me?"

"I've been wanting you, Sunshine. Every time I see you, I want to pull you close. When I leave to go to work, I miss you and look forward to coming home."

She sighed, starting to lean into the gentle hold he had on her. "So it wasn't my coffee?"

"It's you, gorgeous," his smile stunned her, "and your coffee. Now..."

Poppy let out a sigh. "You want the name."

"Let me help you, baby. Let me keep you safe."

It felt like a stone dropped into her middle. Just the thought of saying his name again made her sick to her stomach. "I don't want to say it."

She hated how thin her voice sounded and blinked as tears gathered on her lashes.

Poppy thought she'd have to tug her hands free of his to wipe them away, but Ronan beat her to it. He let go of her hands and cupped her face with his hands and smoothed away any tears that threatened to escape with his thumbs.

"If you don't want to tell me, I can call in a favor at the CCPD and get a copy of the police report. Or I can call Chicago-"

"No." She shook her head. "Don't waste a favor on something like that, Ronan. Don't-"

He kissed her, his lips soothing the argument from hers. "It's not a waste if it's for you."

She shook her head, still trying to wrap her mind around the thought that he wanted to help. That he wanted her.

"I don't want to say his name," she tried to explain, "I've

said it a couple of times already, and I know this sounds... stupid or crazy, but I feel... I feel like saying it again would almost be like black magic... Like I'm-"

"Summoning him?"

"Yes," she blinked back the tears that threatened to fill her eyes, "exactly. I know it's silly, but-"

He pulled her into his arms, and she felt his body warming hers.

"It's not silly, Poppy. You know how you feel. You'll learn to trust that I'm going to be here for you. That I want to know how you feel. To help you and support you. That's what I want to give you."

"That's a lot." She was almost whispering because her throat felt raw with all kinds of emotion. It was a lot for her to take in. "What can I give you in exchange?"

Something passed through his eyes, like a dark cloud in the skies.

"You don't have to give me a thing, Sunshine. You make the world better just by being in it. I want to protect you, no matter what."

"It's just so hard thinking... understanding that you'd do all of this for me and not-" She bit into her bottom lip and shook her head. She didn't want to say what was in her head.

"Tell me, Sunshine." He placed his cheek against hers and spoke softly. "The last thing you'll ever have to worry about is telling me what you think and feel. It makes me want to hurt this guy more thinking that he has you thinking that what happens between a man and a woman is an exchange. Once you start thinking that a relationship is about balancing a scale, that's not love, that's a business."

He leaned back and looked her straight in the eyes.

"I'm going to give you anything you want from me and

more. Whatever you give me from your heart, that's all I want or need."

She looked into his eyes and saw the earnestness of his heart and soul looking back at her.

Poppy had never had that before.

She'd always had to hope for that kind of attention, or for that kind of regard.

Ronan Duncan gave her more in one evening than she'd had from any man in her life. He gave her that open regard and she wanted to give it back over and over again.

Life suddenly didn't look so dark.

"Let me get a pen and paper." She moved away from him and made it to the counter where she reached across and picked up a pen and tore the top piece of paper from her notepad. She set it down before her and saw Ronan lean his hip against the counter a step away.

Poppy had to make herself breathe as she wrote out the name with carefully printed letters. If she made a mess of it, she didn't want to do it again. When she was done, she set down her pen, picked up the notepaper from the very edge and held it out.

Ronan took it from her and looked down at the name she'd written out. She knew the name that he was committing to memory as they stood together in her coffee shop.

Bradley Jansen.

CHAPTER SIX

Ronan looked over at Poppy asleep in her bed.

He was sitting across the room, searching records on his phone.

Seething.

Burning.

If he wasn't sitting in the same room with her, he'd probably have gone straight to his gun safe and tracked down the fucker.

There is nowhere Bradley Jansen could hide. Another city? He'd find him.

Another country? No problem. Ronan had his passport and money to burn.

Where could the asshole go to get away from him?

Not far enough. Not fast enough.

He'd have him behind bars at the least.

Six feet under at the best.

Looking through the documents that Poppy had filed in court, he felt a kind of feral fury race through his veins. Looking through the photos?

He was dangerously close to throwing his phone across

the room as if destroying the images would do a damn thing to erase the fear and pain that Poppy had gone through.

That she'd come back from.

Thinking through the moments of light and joy that she had brought to the darkest corners of his life, he had to wonder how she'd managed it?

And what kind of a man was Bradley to do that kind of damage to anyone, let alone a woman?

"He's not a man," he growled under his breath. "He's a fucking monster."

"You're still here?" Poppy yawned and sat down beside him on the seat she had tucked into the corner of her bedroom. "You should get some rest. He's not worth a sleepless night."

He looked down at his forearm and saw that Poppy was gently stroking his arm. "He's worth losing sleep over because I'm going to protect you."

She turned, bringing her feet up onto the seat next to her, and tucked them under her long nightgown. "You've been working since first thing in the morning and it's..." She looked over at the bedside table. "It's going to be dawn in a few hours," she yawned again and he shook his head, "you should get some rest."

"I like it right where I am."

Her laughter was soft and the sound sent shivers up his spine and sent blood rushing below his belt.

"Okay then." She wiggled down a little until her head was pillowed high on his chest and she wrapped her arm around his middle. "I've imagined this."

He heard the sweet sleepy slur of her voice and felt the way her hand made slow circles over his stomach.

It made him a little nervous and on edge having her touch him like that.

Ronan knew he was a big man. Tall. Broad in the shoulders. Barrel chest. He just wasn't sure if Poppy liked a guy built like him. Where she laid against his side, it wasn't like he could hide his shape, or rather the shape he wasn't in.

"Hmmm..."

She hummed and Ronan wondered if she'd drift back to sleep in a few minutes.

He tried to firm up his belly a little, hoping that she'd fall asleep and he could relax.

He was a man normally comfortable in his skin, but for Poppy, he wished that he was more.

Or maybe a little less.

"Ronan?" Her voice was dreamy and held a little sigh in it when she spoke again. "Why are you so tense?"

Fuck him sideways.

He tried to get his mind in gear and find something clever to say. Or worst comes to worst, he'd just find something that didn't make him sound like an idiot.

Lifting his arm from behind her body, he draped it over her shoulders and drew her closer to his side.

"You've been up for hours."

She yawned and he couldn't help yawning in return. It was contagious.

He lazily rubbed his thumb against the bare flesh of her upper arm. "I've been watching over you."

Poppy snuggled closer and she moved her fingertips across his belly. "I could get used to you touching me like this. Being next to me when the world is quiet like this."

He leaned closer and placed a kiss on the crown of her head. "Just when it's quiet?"

Ronan turned his hand slightly and copied the light, teasing strokes of her fingers with his own hand, teasing the flesh along the back of her arm.

She shivered and leaned in against him, arching her back like a cat. "I know I can't expect you to be with me all the time. You and I have our work cut out for us." She yawned again and then snuggled closer.

If she kept doing it over and over again, she might end up sprawled over his body.

Ronan had no problems with that.

"You know..." She sighed and rubbed her cheek against his chest.

He pulled in a breath as her lips parted and just the slightest brush of her lips against his shirt, just above his nipple, had him aching and hard sitting on her chaise lounge.

She wiggled her body and shifted so that her body was almost straddling his leg.

"Imagine..."

Her words were drifting off and he knew she was half asleep. Or more than that.

"Imagine," she repeated, "if I was doing this for real."

Her normally sweet laugh was throaty and deep as she lifted her half-lidded eyes to look at him.

"You'd be putty in my hands, you know." Her smile was dreamy and wicked at the same time.

She was enchanting.

"Can you imagine that, Ronan? Me, with my hands on you, shaping you like putty?"

The hand that she had on his belly skirted down over his body and then swept down to the middle of his thigh.

"Would you let me put my hands on all of you? Even down here?"

She drew her hand back up toward his hip, but her pinky finger nearly skated along the rise of fabric that was all but strangling his cock.

"I bet you'd like it. I know I would." She laughed and then

giggled when he slumped down under her, hoping to ease the tension.

"Oh, I like it all right. Too much." He groaned and reached down with his free hand to adjust his position in his pants. "You keep touching me like you're doing, Sunshine, and I'm going to need a change of clothes."

Her laughter was playful, but the look in her eyes when she leaned her head back to look at him was an open invitation.

Heaven help him.

Poppy was a temptress.

How was he going to turn her down? Stopping her would kill him, but there was no way he was going to let anything happen between them when she was basically dreaming it.

She grasped his shirt with both of her hands and pulled herself up high enough that her awkward straddle over his leg fit her heat tight against his thigh.

He didn't know what to do, not really. He felt helpless to do much more than watch this beautiful woman settle his leg between hers.

Ronan tried to fight off a cramp in his thigh. He wasn't going to move her off of him. He'd cut his leg off first.

With her hands grasping onto the front of his shirt, she canted her hips against him, and let out a soft moan.

So fucking beautiful.

Poppy rolled her hips and if they'd managed to shed their clothes before this moment, he'd bet he'd feel her hot and wet against his skin.

His dick twitched in his pants and he saw stars in the outer field of his vision.

Her lips were parted as she rocked against him so he could listen to her breaths, much shallower than before, but faster.

Ronan bit the inside of his cheek as she arched her back

and he got a sweet look at the tops of her breasts just beyond the neckline of her nightgown.

Every rock of her hips gave him a new view of her.

Every shift of her hips and squeeze of her thighs around his leg made him just a little harder in his pants.

If she kept riding his leg like this, he was sure he'd come in his pants. And as embarrassing as that might be, he knew he'd suffer through it gladly.

He could already smell her arousal and felt the wet heat seeping through to his bare skin.

What he wouldn't give to wring an orgasm out of her with his mouth on her pussy, but this was her... dream. He was just the lucky SOB to be there to witness it.

An open-mouthed sigh was music to his ears and the grip she had on his shirt popped a button free from his shirt.

His heart was thundering in his chest as he watched her, his hands gripped tight to the edge of the ridiculously dainty piece of furniture.

Her hands climbed higher on his chest, and he saw the point of her nipples pushing against her nightgown. His mouth watered at the sight. He could see the swell of her breasts in the subtle spill of moonlight through the window and he pressed his tongue against the top of his mouth, desperate to keep quiet.

"Oh. Oooh." Poppy moved higher on his leg, her thighs widened, and he felt like her arousal was fire against him. "It... it feels..."

"Fuck." He ground out the word, trying to keep quiet, but he was just a man, and she was a temptress. No. She was a goddess. "You feel so good, baby."

Poppy arched her back and her nightgown stretched across her pretty tits.

It was killing him not to lean closer and suck on her breast until the fabric was nearly transparent.

He just wanted to get closer, but not yet.

Not when she was locked in a dream.

He was horny, but he wasn't trying to be an ass.

"Oh! My go-" Her voice became a breathy gasp, and a moment later she had her eyes wide open and fixed on his. "Ronan?"

He ground his teeth together as he felt her hand grab hold of his shoulders.

"What am I doing?"

"Killing me, Sunshine. Killing me," he groaned, "but I'm loving every damn minute."

He felt her hesitate and her thighs gentle around his leg.

"Don't stop unless you want to stop, Poppy."

"But I'm... it's like I'm using you."

One hand of hers covered her mouth in shock. Before he could think twice about it, he took her hand in his, gently pulling her hand to his lips.

"It's not using me if I'm a willing participant, sweet. I don't want you to stop unless *you* want to stop. If not, I want you to finish. I need you to finish and show me how much more beautiful you are when you're coming apart, squeezing me tight."

He wasn't sure what made up her mind, but he was thankful for it nonetheless.

She leaned in close, one hand gripping the side of his neck, the other fisting in his shirt.

Poppy rocked against him, riding his thigh, and all he could do was watch her, committing every beautiful moment to his memory.

She hid her eyes from him at first, but he couldn't let that happen. Not for long.

He spoke to her.

Soft words. Hungry words. Urging her on to find her release.

He was ready to burst. Ronan had never felt so much pent-up sexual energy crammed into his body before.

All of that with just his thigh between her legs.

His head fell back a little, almost swallowing his tongue as she sank down on him, her body shaking from head to toe.

Ronan felt himself on his own precipice of release and when she grabbed a hold of his beard and tugged him forward, he went willingly.

Her mouth crashed against his as she called out. He swore he could hear the sound echoing in the room, filling his ears with her ecstasy.

He wrapped his arms around her and held her tight as they both came down from the high that they'd found together.

Ronan slid down on the oddly shaped chair, careful to hold her securely against him as her breathing slowed.

She ducked her face down into his chest. "I can't believe you just let me do that."

He stroked a hand over her back, smiling gently to ease his voice. "I'd let you do anything you want, baby. To me. With me. Having your hands on me? Feeling you hot and wet against me? That's heaven."

Ronan felt her shake her head against his chest and then her soft groan of mortification.

"How will I ever be able to look you in the eye again?"

"Easy. You just do it." Ronan smoothed his hand over her hair and settled her against his chest. "You're already beautiful, but when you're coming on me? You're fucking transcendent. Don't hide your eyes from me, Poppy. I love everything about you."

CHAPTER SEVEN

"*I love everything about you.*"
That voice. Those words.
It was a dream.
No. Literally, it was a dream.
It had to be.
There was no way that last night-
"Wake up, Sunshine."
Poppy sat up and stared.
Ronan sat down beside her on the edge of her bed, his clothing rumpled and his smile... Well, his smile made her squirm.
"You're even more beautiful in the morning."
Poppy lifted her hands to her face and hair, grimacing at the tangled mess she found. "Do you need glasses?"
He laughed and it seemed to shock them both.
Ronan's laugh softened, but the warmth she heard in his tone was still there. "No, I don't need glasses. I had surgery years ago."
She looked at him, tilting her head to the side. "I wouldn't

mind you with glasses. You'd have that Professor vibe going on."

He chuckled at her words and handed her the mug he'd been holding in his hands. "Well, I'll find some of my old glasses when we have time to play and see how you like it then."

She thought to hide her blush behind the mug, but when she brought it up to her nose, she looked up at him in surprise. "Earl Grey? How did you-"

He reached up a hand and rubbed at the back of his head. "I looked in your cupboards. I hope that's okay."

Poppy enjoyed a long sip of the perfectly warm brew. "If you make me tea, you can feel free to look in any cupboard you want." She turned and looked at the clock on her bedside table. "It's four. How did you-"

"I see your lights come on around this time."

She shook her head. "Do you ever sleep?"

He smiled at her, and she felt her skin tingle under his direct gaze.

"I sleep. Most of the time during the day if I'm following someone at night."

"Night?" She nodded, feeling like a bit of a goose. "Are you out watching people for your clients?"

He put his hand on her knee, covered by her favorite crazy quilt. She felt the sweep of his thumb against her thigh and warmed to the gentle pressure he put on her leg. "I have my share of cheats that I follow. Their spouses deserve to know what they're doing. A lot of people shrug it off, but when a spouse cheats, it can be a danger to their families."

"Oh, I'm well aware of the danger out there."

Silence fell between them and Poppy felt her stomach clench. And not in a good way.

She took a hold of the blanket and moved it off of her legs.

"I guess I should get moving. People want their coffee and crullers."

"Poppy, hey."

Before she had her feet on the floor, Ronan took her hand and moved to stand in front of her.

"Look at me, please?"

With an exhale, Poppy lifted her chin to look at him with as much of a smile as she could manage.

"I'm going to stop him, okay?"

She nodded because she believed him, but she tightened her hold on his hand, because she wanted him to listen to her too.

"I know you're good at what you do."

"Yeah?" He looked happy to hear it. "How do you know?"

"Instinct," she told him, and was rewarded with his broadening smile, "the same instinct that told me Bradley was bad news. That's why I want you to understand something that's been bothering me since you stepped in to help."

He stepped closer and pulled her up onto her feet.

Tears filled her eyes and while she knew it had nothing to do with sadness, Ronan didn't.

He wrapped one arm around her middle while he continued to hold on to her hand. "You can tell me what it is, Poppy. I'll listen to it."

"Good." She dropped her chin in a decisive nod. "I want you to know that whatever this is we have building up between us, I don't expect you to put your life on the line for me. No matter what, I want *you* to be safe, okay?

"I want you to remember that if you're not around, we won't get to see where this is going. And I really want to see where this is going."

He looked at her, leaning over her shorter frame, his eyes managed to be dark and comforting at the same time.

"Good. Because I know this," he brushed a quick kiss over her lips, "is going to be even more amazing than it was last night."

She blushed furiously, remembering the uninhibited way she'd rubbed against him.

"Then we're agreed," she felt a weight lifting from her shoulders, "that you're going to keep safe so I don't have to worry."

His smile listed to one side. "I'll do what I can to protect myself, Sunshine, because I want to feel your amazing body against every inch of me. But there's one thing you need to know.

"From the moment I saw you, and every night since then, I've had my eyes on you, sweetheart. I've imagined hundreds, if not thousands of things that I need to do to you and the sounds you're going to make when I do them.

"But to do them, I'm going to need you safe and in one piece, so if I need to put myself between you and danger, then that's what I'm going to do."

"Ronan-"

"Fuck, I love the way you say my name."

She shivered with sweet sensations all over her curves. "And I love-"

Her alarm clock rang so hard it almost danced off of the bedside table.

The two of them laughed out loud at the interruption before Ronan gave her another kiss. "Go ahead and get in the shower, sweets. I'm going to go downstairs and get the lights turned on and the coffee started."

She walked toward the bathroom in almost a daze before she stopped and turned back around to see him at the top of the stairs. "Wait! Do you know how to get the coffee started?"

He shrugged and she almost groaned at the way his shoulders moved under his shirt. "I figure I can get something done for you downstairs."

Poppy very nearly floated into her bathroom on a cloud of hope.

– BIG 'N BURLY DUO 2 –

As it turned out, he really didn't know how to get the coffee started.

That comment that he'd made to Poppy wasn't meant to downplay what she did, but damn, he didn't realize that he probably needed a mechanical engineering degree to get things started up in Poppy's Milk & Honey coffee shop.

So instead, he'd tucked tail and apologized when she'd come downstairs.

And then he'd lifted her amazing body and fit it to his while he'd kissed her senseless.

The apology ended up just fine with Poppy walking him through the dozen or so steps to roast and grind the coffee grounds and then brew her heavenly coffee.

He'd declared her efforts well worth the cost of coming to her shop, right before a knock on the front door rattled the glass in the pane.

Ronan gave her a kiss that left them both a little breathless before he sauntered over to the door and opened it up for the uniformed officers on the other side of the glass.

After the two had come in out of the cold, Ronan introduced them to Poppy.

"This is an old friend of mine, Crois St. Cyr. He's assigned to Precinct Four. And this amazing woman is Crois' partner, Pilar Bravo."

"She won't be Bravo for too much longer." Crois gave his

arm a little backhanded smack. "My partner here is going to marry that doctor of hers. She might even consider staying my partner for a bit, just to keep me on my toes."

Ronan barely managed to keep his features neutral as Pilar gave Crois a glare that could melt steel girders.

"I'm not quitting, you jerk."

Ronan shrugged and smiled at the female officer. "If you want, I can turn my back so you can kick his ass."

Crois huffed at his words and lifted his hands as if to say, 'Really?'

"Or maybe," Ronan wrapped his arms around Poppy's shoulders as he handed both of the officers travel cups of her amazing coffee, "I can hold Crois down and let you kick him in the nuts."

Crois groaned and recoiled in what might pass for horror, but Pilar seemed tickled by the idea. She held her cup carefully in her hand so her shaking laughter wouldn't spill coffee out of the little spout in the cover.

Ronan loosened his hold around Poppy's shoulders when she turned a look of abject shock up and into his face. "Don't worry, sweets. Crois and Pilar know I'm only halfway kidding."

Pilar switched her cup from one hand to the other and reached into her pants pocket. She held out the folded papers she had in her hand. "Here's the report from yesterday. I let Kate know we were bringing it to Poppy."

Crois shrugged. "My partner is the stickler for rules. Her brother is an agent with the FBI. Me? I'm the one who's always in trouble."

Pilar leaned in and pointed at the numbers she wrote on the bottom of the page. "That's my number. Feel free to call. Anytime."

Nodding, Crois nudged his partner. "With Roan's schedule at the hospital, Pilar has the craziest sleep hours."

Pilar looked at her partner. "Really? We're going to talk about my sleep schedule? How about you let me get down to the real business here? Hmm?" She didn't wait for her partner to answer.

Ronan looked at Poppy to see how she was handling the exchange. His sunshine was handling it like she'd been doing it all of her life.

Now, it may just be that easy, but he had a feeling that Poppy could put up a shield and protect herself when needed.

He didn't know it through research, he just had a feeling, a gut feeling, that this was a skill she'd learned through experience.

Ronan knew that he'd have to watch her carefully, not because he doubted her, but because he wanted to support her.

Pilar tilted her head toward the far side of the room and Poppy followed her over there.

As Crois rattled on, Ronan kept a surreptitious eye on the women. He just wanted to make sure that Poppy would be all right.

-- BIG 'N BURLY DUO 2 --

Poppy felt like Pilar was everything she wasn't.

Well, with the exception of height. On that, they were very similar.

Pilar was fit and put her life on the line everyday serving the community. Poppy, on the other hand, served coffee.

"Hey? You okay?"

Just the simple touch of Pilar's hand on her arm made Poppy feel better.

The officer had an innate ability to feel empathy. It probably served her well on the streets of Center City. Helping her to connect with people.

That brought a smile to Poppy's lips. "Yeah," Poppy shrugged a little, "I was just comparing the two of us and feeling like I was coming up short."

"How so?"

"What you do for the city and the people who live here? How you serve those around you and then," Poppy grinned, "I kind of do too. Only, while I'm not toting a gun, I have a frother and a damn good bean roaster. Besides," Poppy shook her head at herself, "I'd rather not compare myself to you."

Nodding, Pilar agreed. "There's too much coming at us from the outside world to deal with things like that." Pilar's lips compressed into a thin line for a moment. "I'm sure that Ronan's going to move heaven and earth to keep you safe, but that doesn't mean that you can't help yourself."

Poppy opened her eyes wide. "If there's something I can do with all of this," she skimmed her fingertips down along her side and over her curves, "I'm all for it." She looked over her shoulder at Ronan before she turned back. "He keeps talking about putting himself between me and danger and while I know he's trying to make me feel better, I feel this deep gnawing ache in my stomach."

Pilar rubbed her back gently. "It sounds like an intuition that you're feeling. I'd listen to that."

"A police officer talking about intuition," Poppy mused, "that seems..."

"Counter intuitive?" Pilar's shoulders shook with laughter. "Kind of, but there's a lot of intuition in police work. Learning human nature or trying to? It helps us figure out who might be planning something, ready to cause trouble.

"Like when I'm walking down a street and feel eyes on the back of my neck. Other officers call it 'gut instinct', as if it's not intuition. If you'd like, I can teach you ways of defending yourself that can help if you're ever in a bind."

"I'd like that." Poppy put a hand over her quickly beating heart. "I know this will probably sound silly, but over the last few days, it feels like my life is taking a whole new... a whole new–"

"You don't have to put a name to it." Pilar nodded. "Sometimes when your life changes, it's the best thing that can happen to you." Pilar lifted her hand and Poppy saw the glint of diamonds on Pilar's engagement band. "Getting injured at work, I found myself in the Emergency Room and there was this trauma surgeon... Call me so we can set up some time to work together. Until then, keep your eyes and ears open and if you feel like something's wrong–"

"Believe it." Poppy stepped closer and pulled Pilar into her arms for a hug. "Thank you."

Pilar hugged her back. "You're more than welcome."

Poppy heard a low, deep chuckle behind her.

"Pretty hot, right?"

Poppy stepped back and Pilar folded her arms across her chest. "Seriously, Crois?"

Ronan shoved Crois back. "Don't tempt me."

Crois' smile was a devious one filled with mischief. Before he could get himself in more trouble, both Pilar and Crois' radios squawked.

They listened intently to the alert and when it was done, they turned back toward Poppy and Ronan.

"Go." Ronan offered them his thanks for stopping by and

crossed the room to her side as she waved at the officers. "You okay?"

Poppy looked up at him, enjoying the chance to look at him up close. Enjoyed the heat of his body as he leaned in, and when he brushed his lips across hers, she finally answered him, murmuring her words. "More than okay."

CHAPTER EIGHT

Late in the afternoon, Ronan left to do... something.

He wasn't saying, but honestly, Poppy didn't want to know. It was one thing to be in the dark while she was working, but if he said he was going to do something dangerous, she would have been sick to her stomach until he came back.

Ignorance, in this case, was bliss.

Ecstatic, actually.

When the door opened up and yet another tall, darkly hot, guy walked in, she found herself accepting it easily.

Even better, he walked right up to the counter and placed his CCPD badge on the polished wood so she could see it. "I'm Walker. One of Ronan's friends in the police department. I'm going to be here until he gets back."

"Coffee?" Yes, that was the extent of her dialogue at the moment.

"That would be great, thanks." He reached for his wallet, but she waved him off while she picked up a cup to fill.

"Consider it the baby sitter special." She thought she'd

hidden her frustration well, but she should have known better.

"Don't get upset at the big guy," He gave her a wink. "He's used to working alone on the job. He'll come to us for information, but he'll also bring us information."

"Oh?" Poppy tried not to sound too curious. She wasn't all that interested in gossip, but she found herself eager to hear everything she could about Ronan.

She filled the cup and put the cover on.

"Something to eat?" She gestured at the pastry case. "Sweet? Savory?"

It was the last word that seemed to interest him.

"Mushroom gruyere pastry puff?" She was already picking out two of the puffs before he answered.

Laughing, Walker shook his head. "I like cheese. What can I say?"

She put the puffs on a plate and set it on the counter with a couple of napkins. "Feel free to grab a chair."

Walker looked over his shoulder and nodded. "Is there a favorite?"

She looked at the room, scanning from one side to the other, but she already knew the answer. "The big blue one by the window. That one is pure cushion. I love it."

He nodded, but made no movement besides tasting his coffee. "That's good, really good."

"Thanks." Poppy moved to the sink to wash off the tongs she'd used in the pastry case. "I don't do huge batches with my tiny kitchen in the back."

Walker had taken a bite and was munching happily on the pastry. When he had swallowed the bite down, he wiped at his mouth with the napkin. "With food like that, you should be packing this place."

She bit into her bottom lip before releasing it. "I wasn't

looking to make a name for myself. I was actually just trying to make enough to live. I would think about popular later."

Walker wiped at his mouth after finishing another bite. "This has to do with that guy Ronan's investigating."

Poppy agreed. "Same. i just wanted to put some time and distance between me and..." She let the words drift away. "I was just hoping to avoid drama."

"There's more than enough drama in Center City. At least within the first responder community."

"I bet!" She laughed and then winced a little. "Sorry."

"Nothing to apologize for." He shook his head and took a step away from the counter when a van pulled into the drive between buildings. "Let me step outside for a minute."

Poppy felt a knot form in her stomach.

Before Walker made it to the door, she called out to him. "Be careful."

He stopped with his hand on the doorknob and chuckled. "You're sweet. I see what Ronan likes in you." He winked and stepped outside to talk to the driver of the van.

Poppy took a few steps back and leaned against the counter. She let out a sigh, but couldn't seem to stop the smile that came to her lips.

It was nice to see Ronan's friends and get to know a little more about him through what they said and what she saw.

He was worlds different from any other guy she'd ever met. A universe, no, a black hole from Bradley.

At first she'd chalked up her odd feelings to nerves. He was good looking and sharp. He dressed like he came out of a fancy magazine.

It was sad to say it, but she was impressed with him. What she'd seen as cultured manners was just a slick overlay. She'd been flattered by the attention and so... so eager to feel like she mattered to someone that she'd done everything she could to ignore the warning signs.

Weak. Maybe she'd been weak.

Okay, she'd definitely been weak.

But, she gave herself some credit for putting a stop to it.

The door to Milk & Honey opened again and she cleared her throat and put a smile on her face.

Walker made sure that the door closed behind him before he stepped closer. He gestured over his shoulder at the van. "He's from the security company that Ronan hired. I called him to confirm."

Poppy nodded. "Okay. Ronan mentioned putting up a few more cameras for safety."

The door opened up again and the driver of the van walked inside with a tool belt around his hips and a toolbox in one hand. "You, ah..." He looked down at the paper in his hand. "Are you Sunshine?"

Poppy laughed, her hands lifting to cover her cheeks, but she knew she couldn't hide the brightness of her smile.

She was quickly finding out that the sudden change in her life was deeper than she'd thought before.

Every minute was a new revelation and a new discovery.

"Miss?"

"Yes!" She blurted out the answer and laughed. "I'm sorry. I'm acting like a loon. Yes, I'm... Sunshine."

He nodded. "If you don't mind, I'll get started in the corners of the cafe and then if there's time, I'll do the upstairs."

She gestured at the room and grinned. "Please, do what you need to. Would you like some coffee?"

He shook his head. "Not right now, miss. Thank you, though. Electricity and coffee don't play nicely together."

"Oh, brother." Walker picked up his plate and cup. "I'm going to go check out that blue chair."

Poppy watched as the two men walked away, one to his work and the other to a big blue chair.

Her world was an ever changing place and she loved it.

– BIG 'N BURLY DUO 2 –

With his friends taking turn watching the cafe and Poppy through the day, Ronan was able to finish up his remaining jobs and turn in the reports to his clients. It took most of the day, but by the time he returned to the property, he could see that the new cameras were up. The very visible red blinking lights would go a long way to discourage most people.

Most.

Ronan knew that Bradley wasn't just your average, everyday jerk with a complex and wounded ego.

He already had feelers out with his contacts. There was something squirrelly about the man. He was too polished.

Too slick.

It made his skin itch when he read through the information he could pull up on the man.

There was just something 'off' with him.

He pulled into his parking space behind his building and turned off the engine. When he stepped out of the car, he saw a flare of light coming from the garden bench on Poppy's side.

"McCallen?"

The flare happened again and Ronan heard the harsh exhale from the man in the darkness.

"It's been quiet, man. Nothing but your woman upstairs."

"Yeah?" Ronan felt relief flood through his veins. It wasn't that he'd worried about any real threat while he'd been gone. His friends were good. No. They were amazing and they knew how important Poppy was to him. He hadn't said anything about her specifically, but his friends? They'd said plenty.

Just the fact that he'd asked for help had them curious about Poppy. The rest? They'd just sensed how important this was and folks started to volunteer saying that they'd wanted a chance to meet the woman who he was guarding.

They knew it wasn't just a job for him.

The wood slats on the bench groaned as McCallen got up. He wasn't a tall man, but he was all muscle and muscle meant weight. He reminded Ronan of a professional wrestler back in the day when it was your power that made your name, not a fancy outfit or acting up a certain way.

"Thanks, Don. I'm glad you could come by for a few hours."

McCallen moved into the light from the corner fixture and lifted his lidded cup. "She makes killer coffee." His grin was unfamiliar to Ronan. McCallen scowled even more than he did. "It's leagues better than that swill they serve up at the station. You need someone to come and keep an eye out again, call me."

Switching his cup from his right hand to his left, McCallen shook his hand.

"You keep that lady safe tonight, hmm?"

Ronan nodded. "Yeah. Sure. That's the plan."

Maybe it was the yellow light from the fixture, or maybe it was just McCallen's face that made his smile look a little slanted. "You know, the safest place to watch her would be the bedroom, hmm?"

Ronan rolled his eyes. "Keep your thoughts out of her bedroom, man."

"Just tryin' to be helpful."

"Yeah, well, thanks for being here, but if you're going to talk about that kind of stuff, take a hike."

McCallen shrugged his shoulder and started walking back out to the street. "Take care of your lady-friend, man. She's worth it."

Yeah, Ronan agreed, she sure was.

Ronan let himself in with the key that Poppy had given him that morning and quickly scanned the room for the active cameras. He picked them out easily in the darkness. The angles were good and made the most out of the small confines of the little cafe.

There was a space beside the door where the security panel was going to be. Stephen would come back and finish it in the morning. Until then, Ronan would stay as close by as he could.

He knew that Poppy was worried about him staying with her so much. Even when she'd stopped asking about what he might be missing out on with his business, he knew she was worried about it.

And that felt good.

Being worried about.

By Poppy.

Walker had told him on the phone that he was whipped and Ronan happily told him to, "Fuck it, Walker. Keep that shit to yourself."

He'd known that Walker was right.

It didn't take a fucking genius to tell that he was gone. The only reason why more people didn't know about it was that he rarely saw people. He'd been a bit of a hermit for years.

Having Poppy move in next door had changed that.

Had changed him.

And he fucking loved it.

Doors secured downstairs, he made his way upstairs.

He hadn't talked about it with her earlier, but then again, he'd intended to be home earlier, but he'd been out a little longer than he'd wanted to.

When he made it to the landing and looked up, Poppy's bedroom door was open.

He didn't know if that was a habit of hers, but he was hoping she'd left it open for him. Ronan kept going and reached the top a few moments later.

The wooden plank under his booted foot groaned softly and he heard Poppy's voice from the bed.

"I'm glad you're back." Her voice was breathy and soft. "I was trying to wait up for you, but," she yawned and he set his keys down on top of the dresser, "I didn't realize that I'd be so exhausted from the day."

"Exhausted, hmm?" He crouched down beside the dresser and quickly loosened the laces on his boots. He wasn't going to completely undo the laces, it would make more sense to worry about something like that later. "I can stretch out on that lounge chair if you'd like."

A soft shift of sound was followed by a flare of light from her cell phone beside the bed.

Ronan saw her beautiful, sleepy face pillowed on her forearm.

"I'm hoping you'll come here."

She looked so amazing rumpled with sleep that he wanted to pull back the blankets and strip her bare. The haze of light from her cell phone ended just before the curve of her hip and up popped a mental image of him putting his hands on those hips, holding them, gripping them...

"I need to shower."

Her soft laughter made him hard. It was husky with sleep and sounded like it was just on the verge of a moan.

He wanted her skin against his, but he really did need that shower.

"Do you mind the wait?"

She rolled onto her back and stretched, molding the fabric of her tank top across her nipples.

They were hard and he was dying.

Fucking dying to touch her.

"Fuck me." He turned on his heel and headed for the bathroom.

He didn't even bother turning on the lights. The room was the exact opposite of the bathroom in his apartment, so he dropped his clothes in the hamper, smiling at the idea that his clothes were mixed with hers. He turned on the water and reached for the soap holder.

It was empty.

"Damn it."

Dropping his hand down further, he found the pump of a dispenser. Just a few pushes, and he soaped up his skin. He waited to touch his dick until he was all but done. It was sensitive, his skin aching.

He didn't worry if sex was going to happen. It didn't have to. Sleeping beside Poppy would be enough for him, but that's why he was glad he had a chance to take the edge off of his arousal.

His intent was to soap up and rub one out in a few minutes. With his head filled with images of Poppy stretched out in bed, just a few sweeps of his hand over his flesh was all it took, sending ropes of his cum splashing against the tiles and the soap.

By the time he'd washed the walls clean and dried himself off, he was semi-hard again.

Torture.

That's what he was in for.

And he was going to love every second of it.

When he approached the bed, Poppy's eyes were closed and her body looked still. Ronan reached into the bag that he'd brought over that morning and pulled a pair of boxer briefs out and stepped into them.

As soon as he had the waistband settled in place, he felt a hand on his lower back.

"That was a fun little show." Her voice was soft and sleepy. "You didn't have to put those on."

He turned around and saw her watching him, but her eyes were barely open. "Let me get in on the other side, babe."

She sighed.

Ronan didn't even get to the opposite side, he crawled onto the bed and slipped under the covers. He wiggled his arm under her body and turned her toward him so he could see her face only to find out that she was sound asleep.

He laughed to himself, slightly jostling her, but she stayed blissfully asleep.

Turning onto his back, he held her lightly against his side and covered his eyes with his forearm.

She needed her sleep, so he was glad that she was getting it.

And him?

Well, he was beginning to realize that he needed her more than anything.

CHAPTER NINE

Waking up before dawn was drudge for Poppy. That's why she had an industrial grade alarm clock.

Having Ronan wake her up the morning before was like heaven. Especially with the gift of a warm drink to help wake her up?

So waking up with his warmth pressed up against her back was just another level of heaven.

Until she remembered what had happened the night before.

Or what *hadn't* happened.

She'd fallen asleep.

He'd been in the shower and her mind had been full of so many thoughts and ideas.

And then what?

Nothing!

She'd fallen asleep!

It was crazy.

It was horrible.

No, it was utterly mortifying.

What did a girl have to do to get her V card punched?

She'd done all the stuff while she'd been getting ready for bed. Taking a whole lot of care with her razor and sweet smelling lotions. All so she could fall asleep before... She sighed and the change in her position on the bed brought her backside in contact with-

Wow.

Biting into her lip, she took in a breath and let it go, rolling her hips back, just a bit.

Holy Moly.

That was either an epic erection or the handle of a huge flashlight.

She was hoping for erection.

Poppy laid there quietly for a moment, her mind full of a bunch of different thoughts, plans, prayers. Her thoughts were all so delicious, but they were also just plans.

She was awake now.

And if the ache between her legs was any indication, her body had been painfully aware of the hot hunk of man behind her for the last few hours.

Poppy didn't care about stealth and didn't really try to be sneaky. She wiggled free of the arm he'd laid across her body and when she drew the blanket down his body, she smiled at what she saw.

Ronan Duncan was sleeping soundly in her bed. Bare-chested and boxer briefs meant she could clearly see what his body looked like. Fisting her hand in the sheets at her side, she saw that the red hair on his head was dusted across his chest and down his belly.

Poppy smiled as her eyes adjusted to the darkness of the room and she saw the lighter skin of his belly and the red hair that thickened just south of his bellybutton and disappeared under his waistband.

She was still trying to wrap her head around the idea of having him close enough to touch. All of those hours spent imagining what was under his clothes had been fun, but couldn't quite compete with reality.

His leg muscles made her itch to touch and explore him by touch. Ronan's feet were still hidden by the blanket he'd pulled over them when he'd gotten in bed.

Shifting up on her knees, she scraped her teeth against her lower lips and moved until she knelt at the level of his hip.

A quick look at Ronan's face said that he was still sleeping peacefully.

Poppy reached out and trailed her fingers along one leg from the edge of the blanket at mid-calf, up to his knee. Her fingers retreated to the blanket before she trailed her fingers up again, along the inside of his leg.

When her fingertips brushed the skin of his inner thigh, his breath caught and his body stiffened under her playful touch.

Poppy tilted her head to look at him and saw the heated look in his eyes.

"I thought about doing more," she confessed in a soft voice, "but I wanted to make sure you were okay with it."

Ronan rolled onto his back, one hand tucked behind his head, the other laid across his belly. "Okay with what, Sunshine?"

Poppy rolled her eyes and felt her cheeks flame with heat, so she turned her gaze away from his face. "You know." She hooked her finger under the bottom hem of his boxer briefs and gave it a little tug. The action tugged on something else. "With me, touching you."

When he didn't respond, she turned to look at his face and found him watching her intently.

The heat she'd felt on her face flared again, its flames traveling over her skin.

"There you are," he smiled at her, his eyes focused on her face, "nothing compares to your eyes on me."

"Oh?"

He crooked a finger at her and she leaned in as he braced himself up on his elbow and then up onto his hand. When she came within the length of his arm, he gently held her chin and slanted his lips over hers.

She sighed when he leaned away from her, but she was still drawn to his expression. "Just my eyes?"

He laid back against the cushions and put his hand back behind his head. "Your eyes. Your hands-"

His voice drifted away as her hands tugged at his waistband. Ronan lifted his hips up from the bedding and she tugged it down to the tops of his thighs.

Her eyes were still on him then, looking at that part of him that she'd felt tucked in between them just a short time before.

Poppy blew out a breath and put her hands on him before she could think twice about it.

Warm.

No. His skin was hot against her palm.

It was velvet- The skin was like velvet, gliding between her palm and what lay beneath. And his form, she had no words for what she saw before her, except for... perfect.

Her hands, both of them, tried to wrap around him, and she nearly succeeded, but the thing that gave her the most pleasure was Ronan's chest-deep groan.

Poppy lifted her gaze to his face and saw him press his head back into the pillow, his lips parted.

With her eyes focused there, she tilted her hands and

opened her mouth, dragging the flared tip of his cock across her lower lip and then back, wetting it with her tongue.

"Fuuuuck."

She smiled and shook with silent laughter until he lifted his head to look down into her eyes.

His lips were stretched in a smile. "You keep shaking like that and we're going to be in trouble."

Oh?

She followed his gaze and saw that a milky drop of pre-cum was slowly dripping down from the crown of his cock.

Poppy licked her lips and his cock twitched in her hands.

"Baby, you're going to break me."

She felt like magic. She felt like a goddess. She felt like a woman.

And then she leaned over, collected the drop on the flat of her tongue and followed it up to the source. Once there, she wrapped her mouth over the head of his cock and swallowed.

She'd never considered that it might have a flavor, but once she'd tasted it, she couldn't get enough.

Poppy had her mouth and hands on him, licking the length, tracing her tongue under its flared head. She took him deeper and deeper, needing more of him than she could fit, but it didn't matter.

He mattered.

Those gloriously pained moans.

His fingers in her hair.

That litany of words that fell from his tongue.

"So damn good."

"Fuck me. Poppy... please."

She could hear more but the other words didn't penetrate her thoughts. Poppy had meant to explore, but she was determined to devour.

When he lost his breath and then told her he was close-

"So close, Sunshine. So close. You should-"
She had no interest in pulling away.
Poppy had tasted him and she wanted the rest.
Hungry and happy all at the same moment.

She was almost smiling when she felt him twitch against her tongue, and then she felt him explode over her tongue and against the roof of her mouth.

Poppy wouldn't let him go until she felt his hand on her head, his thumb brushing over her forehead. "I'm spent, baby. Let me hold you."

She started to move toward him, but he leaned in, wrapped his arms around her, and pulled her into his embrace.

The alarm clock on her bedside table peeled its warning that it was again time to make coffee and pastries to feed her customers.

It was so cruel, she decided, but when she managed to scoot to the edge of the bed and set her feet on the floor, she decided to smile.

There would be time for more later, but people needing coffee wouldn't wait. And the man, nearly naked in her bed, lived on coffee, so off she went.

– BIG 'N BURLY DUO 2 –

It was near the end of the day that another friend stopped by and he had some time to go up into his apartment and drop off some of his clothes and pack up more. He wasn't going to assume anything, like asking for some space in her drawers.

Did he love the woman?
Hell, yes.

But he knew better than to make assumptions.

That didn't work well with women. It was the reason why a number of his customers were looking for a private investigator, to find out what was left unsaid between partners.

He knew that this wasn't the time to ask for more from Poppy.

They were just feeling out their emotions and needs around each other. He wasn't about to tip the scales before she was ready for that.

He didn't want this to be like oil in the pan and start a flash fire.

He wanted it to last. He hoped she did, too.

Ronan had just started the washing machine when he heard a series of electronic tones. The door already had a bell on it, but he'd also put a laser in the doorframe.

When the door opened and the laser beam connected, it sounded a tone in his apartment.

A series meant some good business. He was more concerned with a single sound. When Bradley had arrived before, it had been a single entry into the shop.

After a few more tones, Ronan lifted his phone toward his face and swept open the alert screen for the security camera.

A couple of men in business suits were moving into the line and a woman with her small child were finishing their purchase.

Ronan switched to a different angle and saw a kid on a bicycle stop just outside. He stepped off and laid the bike against the wall. He had a box under his arm and took out his phone to look at something on the screen.

Ronan leaned over the machine to set the controls and just as the water started to rush into the machine, sounding hollow and distant, a text activated a quick flash of a light on his phone.

He picked it up from the top of the dryer and saw the message.

SOMETHING OFF
COME HERE

He didn't bother to send a return message. Instead, he grabbed a t-shirt as he ran past the pile of clean clothes that he'd just pulled out of the dryer and pulled it on as he ran down the stairs and rushed out of the front door.

He didn't bother locking it.

And as he ran across the narrow drive between the buildings, he felt the freezing cold on the bottoms of his bare feet.

He could see through the large glass panel in the door and what he saw was red.

Poppy standing shocked and still behind the counter and a young blonde woman holding the teen from the bicycle by the back collar of his shirt.

The men he'd seen earlier were stopped, almost at the corner of the building, their gazes locked on the store.

Ronan pushed the door open, making the bells jingle wildly, but he ignored everything except for Poppy.

He crossed to the counter. "What's wrong?"

She didn't react to his voice. She kept her gaze fixed on the box before her.

Ronan looked at the boy and gave him a look that made the boy turn to hide his face. Ronan heard him speak, even though it was muffled by his posture. "I didn't know, man."

He didn't know.

Didn't know what?

Ronan wasn't going to force Poppy to say anything. He had a feeling that speaking the words would scare her more.

He reached out and grabbed the edge of the box and pulled it toward him.

Picking up the card in the box, he saw the carefully written message across the face of it.

WEAR THIS FOR ME
WHEN I COME FOR YOU

Ronan heard Poppy whimper from her place behind the counter when he dropped the card onto the countertop.

The box contained white lacy underwear.

Poppy met his gaze then.

"You didn't-didn't send that, did you?"

He shook his head "No."

Polly started to cry in earnest then, and he moved around the counter to hold her in his arms.

She turned her face against his chest and held him tight.

Ronan looked up at Josephine Swan, an officer with Precinct Four where Walker, Crois, and Pilar worked. The station was just a few miles from his office and they were good friends to come and help.

Joe, as most of her friends and colleagues called her, looked back at him. "He's babbling, Ronan. He works for a messenger service. Barely in High School, if that. He probably doesn't even know who hired them to deliver the package."

The boy lifted his face and Ronan saw tears streaking his face. "I only got this delivery because another guy got sick and my boss called me in, man! I don't know shit."

Joe shrugged and nodded. She believed the guy.

Ronan was leaning toward that too, but shit, the way Poppy was squeezing him, she was still upset.

He didn't blame her.

That fucker was going to stop torturing her like this.

Joe sat the boy down on a chair and Ronan glared at him.

"Stay in that chair." Ronan knew his voice was loud and some called it scary. He was finally glad for that.

The boy nodded and while Joe kept her hand on the boy's

shoulder, she called into Precinct Four and talked to her sergeant, Kate Turner.

A few moments later, she ended her call. "Kate's coming down. She heard about this through Walker. She wants to take the report so she can turn the info over to Chicago PD."

Ronan nodded. He already expected that Walker Ashley had shared the information with Kate, even though they were in different areas of the same station. Kate was Walker's stepsister.

While they waited for Kate to arrive, Joe locked the front door and turned off the neon sign.

Ronan rubbed Poppy's back in gentle circles and spoke softly into her ear. He had no idea exactly what he said, but he was just desperate to take care of her and soothe her worries.

He was going to be strong for her. Not just in that moment, but for the rest of their lives.

First things first, he had to get this guy to back off.

It was time to pay a visit to Bradley.

A Man to Creep conversation.

And it was going to happen soon.

CHAPTER TEN

After the delivery, the rest of the day left her feeling claustrophobic.

She knew Ronan meant well, but there he was.

That's it.

He was everywhere.

When she turned around, he was looking at her.

When she stepped into the back or the storeroom, he was in the doorway, watching.

By the end of the day, she wanted to snap at him.

Actually, Poppy had snapped at him a few times. She just didn't intend to.

She certainly didn't want to.

He was helping. She knew that.

She knew that he didn't want her to get hurt, but with all the trouble falling down around her shoulders, she felt even worse.

It was one thing when it was just her.

She'd met a whole slew of amazing people who had stepped in to help. Yes, they were babysitting her and the shop, but after that young man had been scared out of his mind for just doing his job, she worried about all the other people around her.

Would they be in danger if... no, when Bradley escalated this?

Poppy stepped into the bathroom for a moment of privacy. Setting the lid down, she took a seat and struggled to work through the stress building up inside of her.

What she was discovering with Ronan was amazing. No, she'd never been a girl who attracted men like him. She'd been so surprised when Bradley had shown an interest and that's why she'd gone out with him.

Thinking it was a good thing.

A surprise.

A gift.

Only to find out it was a curse brought down on her head because she said NO.

Sitting there in the bathroom, she felt like the walls were closing in physically and emotionally. What would happen to this relationship if one of his friends got hurt helping her?

It wasn't just that she was worrying about how Ronan would deal with that. She didn't know if she could look herself in the mirror ever again if something happened to one of Ronan's friends.

A soft knock on the door made her cringe.

Lifting her hands to her face, she felt tears on her cheeks. She used her fingers to wipe them from her face.

"Poppy? Is something wrong?"

"I'm fine. It's okay. I just need a minute."

Was she lying?

Yes.

She just wasn't ready to pour out all of her worries to him. He was already doing so much to help.

It would be selfish to add her own stress on top of it, like a big scoop of brown avocado onto a banana split.

"I'll be out in a moment, okay?"

"Yeah." His voice said he didn't believe her anymore than she did. "I'll be here."

When she heard his footsteps heading out into the shop, she stood up and splashed some water on her face, trying to hide the mess of her face.

She tried to swallow down the knot in her throat, but couldn't seem to make it move.

Poppy knew that Ronan was going to be there waiting for her, but that was the problem.

For all of them.

– BIG 'N BURLY DUO 2 –

Something had shifted between them and damn him to hell, he didn't have a real idea of what it'd been or why. He knew that the atmosphere in the shop was oppressive, like summer humidity in the southern states.

He needed to get his head on straight.

Walking around with his mind in a terrible whirl of confusion?

That wasn't good for anyone. Least of all Poppy.

He had to be on the ball to take care of her. He just wasn't sure he could do that at the moment.

Fuck.

His phone rang and he stepped over to the other side of the room to take the call. The last thing he wanted Poppy to know was any kind of bad news. As tightly as he was wound, she was on edge, like she could jump off a ledge and enjoy the journey down.

"Duncan."

"Kate Turner from the CCPD."

He felt a muscle in his jaw tick. "Something wrong, Sergeant?"

He heard her rough cough of laughter. "What's wrong is that I get a call from Chicago telling me that they went to serve an arrest warrant to your guy."

Ronan wanted to bark back that Bradley Jansen wasn't 'his' anything, but that wasn't important to him.

"How did that go?"

"Peachy."

He heard the acid dripping from her tone.

"What happened?"

"Oh," her sing song tone spoke volumes, "he's so slick. Or at least he thinks so. They had him in handcuffs, and he acted like they were silver bracelets. They were interrogating him and he seemed completely unaffected. He didn't answer questions, just said he would wait for his attorney."

"So, when will we know more?" He wanted to get in his car and drive up to Chicago and *help* the police drag information out of him.

"They say the attorney is on his way. I guess we have to wait for that to happen."

"The wheels of justice grinding slowly and all of that, right?"

He turned his head to one side and then the other, working out the tension in his neck. It didn't help.

Kate's voice cut through the noise in his head. "You want to talk to this guy, don't you?"

"Are you even *asking* me this question, Kate? This man sent her fucking lingerie and told her he's coming for her? Do you think that's an empty threat?"

"What I think and what I know are two different things."

She kept her tone strong as she continued. "What I think is that this guy won't stop until he gets what he wants or..."

"Or?"

"Or he's stopped, Ronan. And while I get how much you want to hurt him, putting yourself in danger isn't going to make Poppy happy. In fact, I bet this whole thing is making her a little freaked out."

"Yeah?" Ronan sighed. "Yeah. I can see that. I've been a little..."

"Suffocating?"

"Thanks for the vote of confidence."

She found something to laugh about in his darker tone. "Sorry, it's just that you're a lot like Rock."

He had a little smile at that. "Comparing me to your man, again?"

"You're both intense. Protective. And you both rock that hunky bulk that give you that dad bod that keeps the girls coming."

He listened for another word, but she didn't say it. "You mean," he offered, "that keeps the girls coming back."

"Hmm?" She laughed again. "That too. Now, if you want to give your woman some room and settle your own curiosity about this creep. I can call and get you into the station to talk to the officers. If you want to see him, that's on you. I can probably convince my friend to let you watch the interrogation at the very least."

He looked over his shoulder and saw Poppy with her head in her hands as a customer walked away.

As playful as she'd been that morning, he could see that the whole situation was weighing on her.

They both needed a little space. And now that Bradley was in custody, they could relax a little.

"Ronan?"

"Yeah." The answer came out of his mouth before he'd made a conscious decision. "Yeah. Make the call. Thanks, Kate."

"Take care of her, Ronan." He could almost hear her smiling. "And invite us to the wedding."

Ronan finally found a laugh. "No worries, we'll save you guys good seats up front."

– BIG 'N BURLY DUO 2 –

Poppy felt horrible. It wasn't about the situation with Bradley. No, Ronan had explained that Bradley was in police custody and he was going to Chicago to watch the interview. Or whatever they were calling it.

She was happy about that.

But she felt horrible that she was happy that she had a little peace and quiet in her apartment.

Ronan was a big guy, and when he was there, it was impossible to ignore him.

She was fine with that, but his... intensity was, well... intense.

Her phone buzzed and she picked it up from beside her plate.

> PILAR: Hey, want us to come and pick you up for dinner?

Poppy shook her head and texted back with a smile.

> POPPY: Just ate, but thanks! That's sweet of you.

> PILAR: Soon then. We'll have you and Ronan over to the apartment.
>
> POPPY: that would be wonderful. Thank You!

No sooner than she set the phone back down, it buzzed again.

Her eyes widening as she looked at the screen again.

> WALKER: Ronan's worried you might be UNEASY to be alone. I said that because he said NOT to use the word scared. But you're a woman, not a kid. So if you want me to come by, just say so. I won't even make you feed me. I'm a big boy when I need to be.

She was laughing as she read his words. It sounded like Walker. She really wanted to meet Pilar's fiancé, Roan, too. Roan and Walker were close in age and Pilar said they *kind of* looked like twins, but that's all that was the same.

The three dots appeared and her phone buzzed again.

> WALKER: You okay?
>
> POPPY: Yes. Thanks. I

The building shook and a flash of light lit up the windows. The air in the room was heavy and thick.

A storm was coming. The news had said something earlier, but she hadn't really paid attention.

She hurried to finish the message before Walker got suspicious.

> POPPY: I think the storm's about to hit. I'll be fine here waiting for Ronan to come back. Thanks.
>
> WALKER: okay.

> WALKER: just know you can call.
>
> POPPY: Careful, people are going to start calling you sweet.
>
> WALKER: fuck, no!

She set the phone back down and wondered how many more messages she was likely to get.

If she had money to bet on it, she would guess that Ronan had called in the cavalry.

It made her feel even worse.

It wasn't his fault that she was such a singular person.

An electric crack filled the air with light, and a moment later thunder sent a shiver through her body.

The storm was going to be on top of her soon enough.

Big storms weren't her thing.

Loud booming noises? No thanks.

Shaking the rafters overhead? Nope. NOPE.

Karma, she decided, was giving her a nice swift kick in her backside.

She'd wanted some alone time.

Well, she'd gotten it.

And now? She hated it.

Hanging her head, she sighed.

"Careful what you wish for," she grumbled to herself, "because it looks like you got it."

– BIG 'N BURLY DUO 2 –

Ronan was just about to hit the Chicago City limits when his phone rang. He looked over at the dashboard and swept his fingertip over the screen to accept the call.

"Hey, Kate, I'm almost th-"

"He's gone, Ronan."

"Wait. What?"

"He's gone. They can't find him at the station."

His laugh was hard. Harsh. "This isn't funny, Kate."

"No, it's not. Heads are going to roll over this. I don't know details because they don't. As best as we can figure it out, he probably walked out during the change of shift. The officer sent to take over watch in the interrogation room said that he let out the lawyer that was there. Bradley Jansen is one smooth talking asshole."

"He won't be saying much of anything when I get my hands on him."

"I'll send someone over to Poppy's place. I'd go, but we have our hands full here. The storm dropped down on us faster than we expected. A few random lightning strikes in town have taken out local power generators. So we're having intermittent blackouts."

"Yeah. Okay." He was already turned around and headed back to Center City. "I'll get there as soon as I can."

Ronan flexed his fingers on the steering wheel and pressed his foot down on the gas. With the storm, the road was nearly empty. He would have to keep an eagle eye on the road ahead and get back safely, because he had a horrible feeling that Poppy was going to need him.

– BIG 'N BURLY DUO 2 –

He'd thought that storm was going to be a problem, at first.

But once he'd gotten to Poppy's apartment, he was happy to find out that the storm had knocked out the power.

The locks that separated him from Poppy took a little work, but it wasn't anything too difficult.

And the alarm system that had been installed? Well, he doubted that it would still work without power.

He'd seen blocks without power on his way to her place and one block blinked out while another popped back on.

The electric company was going to have its hands full.

And the alarm company was probably losing their minds over the sudden outage.

Himself?

He was just fine with it.

Taking off his expensive shoes, he walked up the stairs and entered Poppy's bedroom.

It was a little homey for his tastes, but he wasn't going to stay with her in this dump of an apartment. He was just here to get her and go.

Bradley walked across the floor toward the bathroom. He'd done his research, looking into the city files for the blueprints of the two brick structures on one plot. It was a big help to have those plans when he figured out where the electrical main was for her block.

With his luck, it would just be lumped into the surrounding neighborhood outage.

The flickering quality of the light in the bathroom made the corners of his mouth lift.

Candles.

His woman liked candles.

Bradley was one step away from the door when something flashed behind him.

He whirled around and stared at the phone on the edge of the bed.

Grinding his back teeth together, he read the message.

> RONAN: Sunshine? Coming back to Center City. Kate says she's sending an officer to check on you.

> RONAN: She says there's outages all over the city. And with the storm it might take a bit.

> RONAN: Call Walker, Pilar, Crois... any of them. They'll come sit with you.

Bradley stood there, staring at the screen.

He wanted to throw it out of the window, but that wouldn't help him in the long run.

He had to think about what his decisions would mean for them both. He was going to have his Poppet and... feast on her too.

Bradley searched his memory, trying to remember the code she'd used to unlock her phone.

They'd been at dinner and she'd gotten a text from someone. She'd unlocked her phone and when he'd asked her what the code was, she'd laughed at him. *"Oh, I'm not going to tell you. But it's easy to know if you knew me back in college. It's my dorm room phone number."*

She thought that she'd been cute.

Witty, even.

Maybe she thought that he'd let something like that go. But he wasn't like that.

She'd issued him a challenge.

And he'd succeeded.

Looking down at the phone, he dialed in her dorm phone number.

The screen unlocked and he opened up the text app.

> POPPY: Don't worry about me. When the power went out, I called an old friend and they came to pick me up and take me to their place.

> POPPY: Oops. Phone dying. Forgot to charge. Going to shut it off to save what's left of the battery.

> POPPY: See you tomorrow if the storm lets up.

He saw the three dots dance at the corner of the screen and added one more message.

> POPPY: You don't have to worry about me anymore

His finger hovered over the send button, but he didn't send it. Not yet.

He read over the last message and knew that he shouldn't send it.

If that asshole thought she was giving him the brush off, he'd probably come over and see her.

Why?

Well Bradley had done that when she'd told him they weren't going to see each other anymore.

He'd come to see her because he cared.

And that muscled ginger that thought he had a right to Poppy? It was obvious that he cared. So he had to tread lightly with the message.

He could gloat later.

When he hit send, the final message was much better suited to the situation.

> POPPY: Don't worry about me. I'm right where I want to be.

That's when he shut down the phone. Dropped it on the ground. And kicked it under her bed.

He didn't want anyone interrupting their fun.

CHAPTER ELEVEN

P oppy stepped out of the tub, carefully. It would be just her luck that she'd slip and fall and knock herself out.

She'd never hear the end of it from Ronan.

No. He wouldn't scold her for it, but he'd probably never let her out of his sight again.

Being a klutz wasn't one of those qualities that she wanted to exude.

So, instead, she carefully aimed her feet to hit the rug beside the tub.

Perfect.

She took extra time toweling off her body, thinking of what she'd say, *and* what she'd do when Ronan came back.

Her emotions had been all over the place, with Bradley coming back into her life.

Hearing that he was in custody gave her a moment to breathe.

That meant that she could tell Ronan what she'd been feeling. He deserved to hear the truth and all of her silly, dorky thoughts.

He deserved to know what kind of a mess she was. That was only fair to give him the chance to back off and think.

Poppy finished toweling herself off and reached out to drop the towel over the bar along the wall.

"I was hoping you'd let me help dry you off, but I did enjoy the show."

Poppy stumbled back against the wall and tried to yank the towel off of the bar.

It was stuck somehow and she yanked on it again.

"Don't bother covering up, Poppy. It's just you and me, and I'm dying to see what you've been hiding from me."

With one more vicious yank on the towel, she pulled it free and stumbled back from the force. "What are you doing here? You're supposed to be-"

"In Chicago?"

He laughed and her hands fumbled with the over-large bath sheet.

"Yes," she ground the words out from between her clenched teeth, "they said that you'd been arrested for breaking the temporary-"

"That's the thing, Poppet, it was temporary. Now," he stepped closer, lifting his hand toward her face, "it's over, because you're going to tell them that you want to be with me."

She wanted to yell in his face. She wanted to scream for help.

But she couldn't do either of those things.

She was all but naked and a quick look out through the wide picture windows told her that the world outside was still dark.

"You should really go now." She struggled to keep her composure, her hands gripping the towel closed over her breasts. "Ronan will be here at any minute. Before he gets back you should-"

"Your man is likely stuck in traffic. He sent you some text messages."

Her eyes widened at that. "How? Did you read them?"

He shrugged at her with a sickeningly sweet smile. "I even replied back a few times telling him that you were off with a friend and you'll probably see him tomorrow."

Her heart stopped in her chest even as her mind tried to puzzle through his words. "How did you... I mean I guess you saw his messages from my notifications, but there's no way... NO WAY that you sent him anything back."

She lifted her head, jutting her chin out as she gave him a pointed look.

"You're just trying to make me give up. Well, that's not going to happen."

"Give up?" He shook his head. "Hardly, Poppet. I told him not to look for you tonight. And-" He stopped short and she saw his eyes narrow on her in warning. "And if you must know. It wasn't all that hard to get your old dorm phone number. A couple hundred dollars to some scholarship kid in the office and a sappy story of unrequited love." He snapped his fingers. "Voila! I guess you didn't change your password after we talked about it." He gave her a smile that looked more like the slanted smile of a ravenous wolf. "You'll learn, sooner than later, if you're a good little girl, that it's easier to listen to me. And make me happy."

He put his hands on her shoulders and gave her a gentle squeeze.

"You understand, don't you, Poppet? When I'm happy, I'll make you so happy."

Bile rose up in her throat.

She didn't know what to do.

She couldn't quite summon up the energy to do much more than stand still, watching him.

"Now," he smiled and looked at her with as much affection as she believed that he could muster, "you're going to go and put on my gift. And then grab a coat so we can leave."

His gift?

The lace lingerie?

As she stood there, she could see his expression change.

Harden.

"Put on my gift, Poppy."

"It's with the police. When the delivery came, it went with the police who came to take the statement, and-"

Lightning exploded in her head, rocking her back with the force of his slap.

Her vision blurred and when she saw his hand coming at her head again, she couldn't quite stop him.

His fingers fisted in her hair, still somewhat damp from her bath, and by the screaming pain that lanced across her scalp she knew that he'd pulled some of her hair from her head.

His voice was close enough to her ear that she felt his breath against her skin.

"You gave away my gift?"

She wasn't at all sure what she could do to placate him at this point. Did she want to dress up for him? No. But she also felt like she didn't have a chance if she didn't find a way to make him happy.

"They... they took it when-"

That's all she got out before he grabbed her towel and yanked it away.

Poppy stumbled forward and ended up on her hands and knees.

She pulled in a breath, hoping to steady herself and think

clearly. Poppy braced herself on her hands and started to get a foot under her.

He pushed her down and the impact on her knees sent waves of pain up through her thighs and into her tailbone. She whimpered under her breath because her teeth had caught the edge of her tongue.

"I didn't say to get up!"

His voice was loud and he sounded happy with her posture.

Before she could think of anything to say, she heard the sound of leather snapping. Poppy turned and regretted it a moment later.

Bradley had his belt in his hand and, as he brought it down toward her, she didn't have time to turn away.

The leather slapped against her upper arm and back, the sound of the strike echoing in her bedroom.

"What did you do?" His voice was thick with emotion. "Don't be so stupid! If you look at me, I might strike your face!"

She bore too much pain to speak back to him. Her back and the tender skin of her arm felt like they were on fire.

"Look down at the floor!" He ordered her. "Let me punish you and then we can leave. I'll buy you more gifts when we're gone from here."

What else could she do?

He had all of the advantages at that moment.

She could bear the pain and try to figure out how to endure enough of it and give Ronan time to come home.

Poppy dropped her gaze to the floor, but another stinging slap landed on her back.

"I'm... I'm looking down!"

He moved closer and she felt his bare hand on her back. "You weren't quick enough, Poppet. Now be a good little girl so I don't have to hurt you much more."

She felt the tears spill from her eyes and fall to the floor.

Her only thought at that moment was for Ronan.

If Bradley wasn't lying to her and sent messages to Ronan? Was there any way that she'd get out of his?

She hoped so, but worry might be all she had left.

– BIG 'N BURLY DUO 2 –

When he got home, he tossed his keys in the dish beside his front door. He pulled his phone out and looked at the screen. No new messages.

For a moment, he considered turning on his tracking app to see where she was, but he'd already been smothering her since her ex had that package delivered.

Ex.

Bradley wasn't really her ex.

Two dates didn't make a boyfriend.

So it didn't make an ex.

Right?

Well, he hadn't even taken her out on a date, so where did that leave him?

Them?

Fuck.

Ronan looked around the bottom floor of his apartment. Unlike Poppy who'd used her storefront as a cafe, he'd just boarded his up.

He didn't need a storefront to be a private investigator. He just needed his brain, a decent computer system, and contacts all over the place. It might have been fun to dress up like Mike Hammer and have a massive wooden desk, but he didn't bother with it.

Without thinking, he reached out his hand to flick on the

lights before he remembered that their block was part of the nearly fifty percent outages around Center City. Leaving the switch alone, he walked up the stairs to his apartment.

With an awkward smile, he shook his head.

When was the last time he'd spent the night at his apartment alone?

Had it been just a few days?

He couldn't imagine his life going in any other direction other than toward Poppy.

Now that he'd gone from watching her from the darkness of his apartment to spending the night in her bed, he couldn't go back to living his life alone.

It was just impossible.

He was fucking head over heels for Poppy and he had to do what he could to work things out with her.

Up in his apartment, he yanked off his shirt and tossed it onto the chair that sat in the corner of the room.

It was the same chair where he'd sit sometimes and watch Poppy in her apartment. He sat down and worked on the laces of his boots. Ronan wasn't in a rush. There was no need to hurry, just to end up in bed alone.

Once they were loose, he toed off the boots and sat back in his chair, staring across the divide between the two buildings.

Her apartment was dark and it affected his mood.

He just had a feeling.

A really bad feeling.

Picking up his phone, he dialed Poppy again.

Straight to voicemail.

Damn it!

Ronan tried the Find a Phone App. As it opened up, he went back to his Messenger App and read through her last few texts.

Then he went back to the other application, with his

thoughts focused on the idea that he'd at least know where she was when she turned it off.

The area where her friend's place was.

That would take some of the edge off of his worries.

The screen opened and showed his phone in his apartment.

Not what he wanted.

So he expanded the map, pinching the screen down so that his indicator was just a tiny pin of light on the screen.

Still, nothing.

Back to the texts, he looked at the time that passed between her messages. It didn't seem like she'd gone far.

He lurched out of his chair and paced before the big picture window, trying to work his mind around the worry that he was missing something.

Something he should know.

-- BIG 'N BURLY DUO 2 --

Another crack of his belt across her back blinded her eyes with tears.

She cried out, but she also grit her teeth together to hold in the pain.

As much as she hurt, she had a feeling that Bradley would enjoy her pain more than her silence. So she'd keep trying to ignore it as long as she could.

No, not ignore.

Endure.

"I'm going to be so good to you, Poppet. You're going to love the way I treat you."

Something broke inside her.

She didn't have time to wait.

Did have time to hope.

For all she knew, no one would come to look for her until it was too late and he'd broken her soul.

When she felt him shift backward, she moved.

She wasn't as fast as she could have been without the painful welts across her back, but she was fast enough to surprise him.

Poppy grabbed at his arm, determined to keep the leather strap from her skin, but he had a hold of her hair and he wasn't about to let go.

So she fell against Bradley, unable to get away with his fingers twisted into the back of her hair, and the two of them crashed into her lamp.

At least that's what she thought, by the sound of shattering glass. Her faux-Tiffany stained glass might just cut them both up, but it was her chance to get on top for a moment.

And she wasn't going to let it go to waste.

She felt around on the ground, glass cutting into her palms, searching for the tube of the lamp.

"You bitch!"

Bradley made a glancing blow on her shoulder, but she couldn't do much to move away from it. She needed to fight for the upper hand, but Bradley's strength was chipping away at her own.

"I should just-"

The air was suddenly exploding over her head.

Sound, air, and glass swept through the room. The pressure of it all threw her sideways and off of Bradley.

She rolled onto her back, slamming against the wall behind her.

That's when she noticed that the air around her was filled

with moisture, rain flying through the space and fluttering the curtains around what was her picture window.

– BIG 'N BURLY DUO 2 –

He'd heard the shattering glass in her apartment moments after he'd zoomed in closer on the application and seen that Poppy's phone's last message had come from her apartment.

Instinct took over.

Instinct and rage.

There wasn't time to shove his feet into his boots or grab up his shirt.

He reached out to his dresser and picked up the pistol he'd left there. That, he tucked into the back of his pants as he backed up to the far side of the room and ran, full out, right through the window and across the narrow drive between their apartments.

Her window gave easily, imploded from the impact of his body.

And then he was there, standing in the middle of her bedroom, taking in the scene before him with the barest glow of the moon filtered through the rain.

Bradley and Poppy surrounded by pieces of glass, the asshole with one hand wrapped around the doubled strap of his belt. And even in the soft light from the moon, he could see a pink welt on her shoulder and that's when the pieces fell into place.

Somewhere deep down inside him, he lost control.

"You fucking animal!"

Ronan picked him up by the front of his shirt, but stopped when he saw Poppy's pale golden hair in the man's fist.

He lowered Bradley down and heard Poppy's sigh of relief.

Ronan gave him a shake. "Let her go."

Bradley just stared at him, wide-eyed.

Ronan twisted his hands in Bradley's shirt to the point that his face paled noticeably. "Let her go, or I kill you right here."

"Ronan-"

He could hear the trepidation in Poppy's voice, but he knew what he was doing.

He knew what he wanted to do.

They might end up being the same solution.

Maybe.

He took the pistol from the waistband of his pants and shoved it up under his jaw so deep that he wasn't sure that Bradley could breathe.

"Let. Her. Go."

Ronan knew the moment that Bradley let go of her hair, because she moved back and out of his reach.

He wanted to turn around and look at her.

He wanted to turn around and talk to her.

But he knew if he saw a tear in her eye or saw another welt on her skin, he'd murder Bradley.

Not in cold blood.

No, if he killed Bradley at that moment, it would be hot blooded fury. He'd battered people before. Beat them to within an inch of their lives for the horrible things they'd done.

This was different.

This was Poppy.

His sunshine.

The woman he loved.

There might not be enough of Bradley to identify if he did it right then.

"You have one chance to live through this, Bradley." Ronan sneered his name. "You have to tell me. Give me one reason why I shouldn't rip you right down the middle and toss you into a trash bin where you belong."

It was really something to see.

Bradley was a man on the verge of passing out, he might even have seen his life passing in front of his eyes, but all he could do was stare right into Ronan's eyes with a cold glare.

"Give me a reason, *Bradley*. Now."

Ronan relaxed his hold on the neck of Bradley's shirt so he could manage to take in a full breath.

"Tell me something that might save your life."

Bradley's eyes were full of hate and his pupils were like pinpoints. "I want to fuck her so damn bad. You can watch if you like." His smile was sadistic. "Maybe I'll let you have a turn."

Ronan felt Bradley's nose break against his knuckles.

He lost that smile in a heartbeat.

Ronan pulled his fist back, ready to punch Bradley's nose into his face.

"Do it, you stupid fuck! Do-"

"Ronan, stop. Please."

He turned then.

He turned toward Poppy and saw the fear in her eyes. It wasn't for Bradley.

She didn't even look at the man who'd attacked her.

Poppy was looking at him with love and hope in her eyes.

He'd never be able to turn her down. To deny her when she had her heart in her eyes like that.

"He hurt you."

She swallowed and he watched the pale column of her

throat work through her answer. "But you're here now, Ronan. You're here and that's all that matters to me."

"Okay..."

Ronan heard Bradley speak, but he didn't bother looking at him.

"I'll let you fuck her first."

Bradley's head snapped back when Ronan's fist connected this his jaw.

He was out cold before Ronan lowered him to the ground.

Ronan swept Poppy up from the ground and carried her toward the bed. Yanking the blanket off of the top, Ronan sent the old sheet and glass shards down onto the ground and all over Bradley.

When he set her down, he moved his hands over her body, gently searching her beautiful body.

"He hurt you."

"I don't care about that," she reached for him, wrapping her hand around his and drawing him closer. "You're here."

Cursing under his breath, he held her gently in his arms. "I left you alone."

"He was in custody."

"He slipped out of interrogation. Heads are going to roll in Chicago."

Ronan leaned back and looked into her eyes, "I could probably make a case for him 'falling' out of the window."

"No!"

He heard the dismay in her voice and shook his head. "I won't, but I want to think about it."

"I have better things to think about than him," she set him straight. "I've got you."

"You've got me, Sunshine. Just know that I'll never fail you again."

"Fail me?" He could hear shock and outrage in her voice.

She turned her head and he followed her direction. Noticing the mess he'd made out of her window. "You came through that window?"

He shrugged. "I had to get to you, Poppy. I couldn't let him take you from me."

"I fought him too, Ronan. I wasn't going to leave you without a fight."

He kissed her, holding her body like she was made of glass. When he pulled back, he was barely an inch away from her luscious mouth. "No more fighting, just love. You and me."

She cuddled against him, her arms around his middle. "I like the sound of that." Poppy leaned her cheek against his shoulder. "I love you."

"I love you like crazy, Sunshine. So crazy that I need to put in a call to CCPD to get them to come out and take Bradley's ass to jail. Then I've got a friend in the Fire Department who does some construction on the side to come and board up all these windows.

"And while he's doing that, I'm taking you to Cole Medical to make sure you're okay."

"We don't have to go to the Emergency Room," she sighed and grumbled a little. "I've got some salve that I can put on it. The last thing I want to do is spend half the night waiting to be seen."

He looked at her, searching her expression. "Okay, so if we don't go there, I've got another idea."

"Oh?" Her smile lifted the corners of her mouth. "What?"

"A hotel. Silky soft sheets. Downy soft blankets. And the chance to hold you in my arms for the rest of the night."

He saw her smile brighten, but he also saw a spark in her gaze, too.

"I love that idea, Ronan."

"And I love you, Poppy."

CHAPTER TWELVE

Things progressed quickly after the police arrived at Poppy's apartment. The Crime Scene Investigation unit were all busy at other calls, but Kate Turner showed up and did a triage of the scene so that Gibson Braun, a lieutenant from Station 29, could board up the matching busted windows of their apartments.

Kate hadn't come alone, she'd brought her man with her.

They called him Rock at the Fire Department, but Ronan couldn't remember much about him. He was sure they were living together, but he couldn't remember if the two were shacking up or married. He knew Kate through his work, Rock, not so much.

Kate knelt down beside Poppy, her hand on Poppy's knee. Ronan moved closer, not that he was concerned by what Kate might say, but he just wanted to be closer to her.

"I'm fine, but Ronan McSurly wants me to go to the ER."

Ronan raised a brow at the comment but didn't say a word. The fact that Poppy was almost fighting mad made him feel better.

Poppy gave Kate a look at her back, allowing her to take

photos for the police report, before she pulled her robe back on.

Kate shrugged. "It would be good to get someone to look at your back."

Ronan grinned at the Sergeant's assessment, but his grin didn't last long when Kate continued.

"I happen to know a Trauma Surgeon."

Poppy's eyes widened at her words, but Kate explained further.

"My brother, Roan Ashley, works in the ER. He's off tonight, so he can come by and check on you."

Ronan opened his mouth to accept, but he felt Poppy's hand on his arm.

He looked down at her.

"Ronan, I don't want a doctor. I just want you."

Fuck.

How could he refuse?

The hotel let them come in the side door to avoid curious eyes and the manager met them and escorted them up to their room.

When Poppy got a look at the room, she stared. "How much did this cost?"

She turned her worried gaze to him, but he held her gently by her shoulders. "Don't worry, Sunshine. You leave that to me." He placed a gentle kiss on her forehead. "Seriously, though. I could easily afford a room here, but the manager is a former client of mine. He offered to give us a place to stay while we get our windows fixed."

As he spoke, his hands touched her face,

"And I wanted you to have a place where we didn't have

to worry about the power going out. Here, you won't have to worry about him coming after you."

As his hands smoothed down the column of her neck, she gave him a watery smile. "I'm not."

His hands caressed her shoulders and arms, slowly and oh so tender. "I let you down."

She shook her head and crossed her arms over her chest, laying her hands on his. "You saved me. You jumped through panes of glass to save me. How is that failing me?"

Humbled.

Broken.

So fucking in love.

That's how he felt.

"I should-"

"Don't." Her expression changed and he saw a frustration inside of her eyes. "Don't talk about should."

When he didn't answer, she brought her hands up between them, smoothing her palms from his shoulders to his stomach and then around to his waist.

"What I want to think about is this, Ronan. You. Here with me. You warm and alive against my hands."

She leaned closer, wrapping her arms around him until her cheek pressed against his chest and her hands pressed against his back, holding him tight.

"Your heart beating in your chest, feeling the vibrations against my skin."

Poppy pressed closer and Ronan groaned, she was so close to him and when he breathed in her scent, he felt as if she was inside him.

Filling him up from the inside out.

"He laid his hands on you."

"And you were there."

"He could have killed y-"

She kissed him.

No, she fought off his demons.

She pushed them away with the tender searching touch of her lips.

Poppy's hands soothed away the tension in his shoulders and ignited the flames of passion that had been blanketed by fear.

Before his mind could wrap itself around what was happening, he felt her hands slip down over his belt and her fingers dug into his ass.

Poppy turned her head and pressed a kiss on his chest.

And then another, before she tipped her head back to look into his eyes.

"Don't doubt that you saved me, Ronan. But, you didn't just save my life. You made it better. Having you here, with me? I've never been so happy."

She rose up and placed a kiss at the base of his throat.

"I hope I can do the same for you."

Shit.

He'd never been so hard.

Ever.

"You can, baby."

Her eyes widened and her pupils dilated as her breaths shallowed. "How?"

– BIG 'N BURLY DUO 2 –

When she asked the question, she had no real idea of what he meant. She was almost sure she was going to blush when he answered.

Poppy was absolutely sure that she'd love it.

Well, Ronan didn't tell her.

He showed her.

Oh, did he show her.

Somehow, Ronan was able to strip her bare without a single twinge of pain in her back.

And then he coaxed her on the bed, bare all over.

He was there a moment later.

On his back.

Urging her forward, he braced his hands on her thighs so she could straddle his face, and he used his fingers between her legs to widen her stance.

Anticipation.

It was anticipation and not curiosity that would kill her.

"Ronan, I-" She sucked in a breath when she felt him kiss her... there.

"Oh..."

Then she felt his tongue sweep against her folds.

"Oh..."

Poppy had her hands on her hips because she didn't know what else to do.

"Oh!"

His hands reached around her thighs and drew her down. Fitted her over his mouth.

His tongue drew breathy cries from her lips and the bristly brush of his beard against the flesh of her inner thighs made her shiver.

She dropped one hand down and combed her fingers through his ginger hair.

Oh, yes.

She'd heard about the act, but to have Ronan's mouth feasting on her from below, his hands pulling down on her thighs to hold her tight against him.

He was ravenous and her mind whipped back and forth between the amazing rush of pleasure through her body and the worry that she would likely smother him when she lost control.

And that moment, was growing closer and closer as Ronan dragged his tongue through her folds and turned his head until he was able to circle her clit.

"Oh! Holy-"

She shot up and leaned forward as if she might fly right over him.

Ronan turned his head and brushed his damp beard and tender lips against her inner thigh. "Give it to me, Poppy. Give me all of you."

She let him pull her down against his face and as his tongue swept over her clit, drawing it into his mouth, Poppy felt his fingers slip inside of her sex.

Poppy lost herself in his touch.

Her hips rocked against his mouth, riding through her orgasm as her head tipped back and his name was torn from her throat.

If it was possible to memorize a single moment of sensation, she would certainly pick that one.

All she could feel was the twitch and contractions of her muscles, the flood of sensations that were washing over her.

Somehow, she ended up draped over his body, her head on his shoulder as his hands smoothed over her bare skin and combed through her hair.

"So beautiful," Ronan pressed a kiss against her hair, "I've imagined this. Imagined you."

Poppy managed to lift her head and look at him. "Imagined us?"

His smile made her ache and throb all over again. She loved the way his face seemed to brighten at her words. "Countless times."

She placed her hands on his shoulders and sat up, her legs stretched around his hips.

Poppy knew that thick length pressed against her belly was hard and at the ready. And she was ready to have him inside her.

So damn ready.

Poppy gave him a hungry look. "Well, I don't know about countless..."

"Oh?" He didn't look the least concerned.

No, the amazing man laid out beneath her in bed, reached between them and fit the head of his cock against her. As wet as she was, her body drew him inside until he was nestled in her body.

He shuddered beneath her, the vibrations of his body within hers sent those same sensations through her body.

Ronan had his hands on her hips, holding her in place.

She saw his eyes darken as she tried to sit back and seat herself on his cock.

"I want it to count every time we're together, Poppy."

His hands on her hips pressed her lower and she felt like she might faint at the delicious stretch of her body around him.

"Feel that, love? That's what I want, to fill you. To hear your moan and beg for more."

He drew her down until they were fit perfectly together.

Before she made the conscious decision to move, she was rocking against him, searching for that same desperate high that they'd shared moments before.

When she was breathless with desire, his hands took over, his feet planting on the mattress so he could thrust deeply into her, lifting her higher inside and out.

Poppy had no fear that she'd falter on her climb toward ecstasy.

No, Ronan would carry her over into the wild abandon of release.

"Hold onto me, Poppy. I'm going to bring you to the edge and together," he growled as he plowed deeply into her body. Her fingers bit into his shoulders as she discovered new heights together.

"Yes, love," his breaths punctuated each uplifting thrust, "just like that. Come for me, Poppy. Bathe me in your release."

She had no idea how to make it happen.

Her body just didn't work that way at all, but Ronan's knew enough for both of them.

When they fell into the waves of their passion, neither one had to hurry about how to reach the surface again.

They helped each other rise as they would do for the rest of their lives.

EPILOGUE

How strange it was.

Poppy silently laughed to herself.

Just a few weeks ago, she had no idea that the man who lived across their drive would seamlessly fit into her own little world.

Looking up at the jaunty jingle of the bell above her shop's front door, she rolled her eyes as Ronan's broad shoulders all but blocked out the sun.

When the door closed behind him, she sighed aloud and pulled a plate from the warmer.

By the time Ronan made it to the counter, she was flushed with heat and it wasn't from the cinnamon rolls on the plate she touched with her fingertips.

"It's about time you got here, handsome. I was about to give these to the next brawny, bearded man who walked in the door."

She'd no sooner said the words when the bell above the door jingled again, and she leaned to the side and stared.

A man, very much the same height and Ronan's breadth,

stepped into the shop and lifted his chin in greeting. "It smells like heaven in here."

Poppy beamed with joy. "Thank you. Would you like something to drink? Some pastries?"

He gave his middle a pat and sighed aloud. "I better not, with the pastries. But coffee? Yes, please." He took a few steps forward and nodded as he looked around the shop. "The larger the better. I have to get to work in a few hours."

Poppy paused with an empty travel cup in her hands. "In a few hours? Usually we get folks coming in on their way to work."

Ronan stepped behind the counter and picked up a set of serving tongs, and put a sugar bun on a plate. He brushed a kiss on Poppy's temple as they moved around each other in the narrow area behind the counter. "This is Vincent Kane, love. You've admired his work online."

Poppy gasped as she paused with the travel cup nearly filled to the brim in one hand and a cover in the other. "Oh, yes!! I love your black and gray work! If I wasn't a wimp around needles, I'd come in and get a tattoo."

Vincent Kane's smile was a little hesitant when she held out the travel mug toward him.

"I'd say that I'd be happy to work with you," his gaze drifted to the side and Poppy felt Ronan move closer, "If I didn't think your man might be tempted to rip off my arm."

Ronan's arm settled over her shoulders. "I wouldn't go *that* far."

Poppy elbowed him with the arm that held the coffee lid before she covered the travel cup and gave it over to Vincent. "He wouldn't dare, not with how much I love your work. Still, I'm not at all comfortable with needles, so I'll just have to stick with admiring your work on social media."

Vincent drew in a breath over the cup and nodded his

head. "I think I'll be coming back here if it's only for the coffee. I bet this tastes as great as it smells."

Poppy's cheeks warmed from his kind words. "We have a loyal and dedicated customer base. Just like your shop, Mister Kane."

He shook his head. "Vincent, please."

Ronan introduced her by name before he gestured at the building across the narrow driveway. "Did you get a chance to look at the specs I sent you over email?"

Vincent nodded. "I like the apartment being over the shop. And the security you have in place is state of the art."

Poppy felt Ronan draw her closer against his side.

While she didn't have any nightmares about the experience, she felt comforted, not just by the security system they had, but also Ronan's presence.

"I'd like to take a look at the other building if that works for you." Vincent looked at them both. "I'm not quite ready to make a break from my partner, but the time is coming."

Poppy shared a look with Ronan, concern filling her chest. "Is everything okay? We see a lot about Ink Envy on social media. Business seems to be booming."

"Oh, business isn't the problem." Vincent took a big sip of his coffee and sighed. "It's the man I'm in business with. Things have been up and down with him for a good while, but if... if things don't get better, I wanted to look around and see what spaces might be open."

The warmer dinged softly and Poppy felt Ronan step back. When he came back up to her side, he leaned in for a kiss against the side of her neck. "I'm going to take Vincent over to look at the building. Take good care of yourself, sweetheart."

Poppy rolled her eyes, but that only made Ronan laugh.

She handed Vincent a napkin before Ronan gave him the sugar bun. "Take this and eat as you go."

He looked surprised, but he gave her a thoughtful smile. "Thank you."

Poppy waved him off. "Enjoy it."

As Ronan and Vincent left the shop, heading over to Ronan's building, she couldn't help but smile.

That, and pick up her iPad to quickly power it up and visit the Ink Envy Facebook page.

As she looked at the page she grinned. There was an album of photos that had been recently added.

INK ENVY STAFF

As Poppy paged through the images, she bit into her bottom lip. There were a lot of pictures of Vincent's business partner, Hannibal Baldwin.

Apparently, he'd never met a photographic device that he didn't like.

She sighed and shook her head. "There's something about that man... yuck."

As she continued through the photo album, she started to notice a few things. The staff of the Tattoo Shop included a rather attractive young woman who was labeled, rather disturbingly as 'Hannibal's Shop Bitch.'

Then, just under that post, a post by Vincent making no bones about the fact that the woman was an apprentice in the shop.

Narrowing her eyes at the screen, Poppy saw that wherever the young woman was, Vincent wasn't far away.

His expression and his body language spoke volumes.

He didn't like his business partner very much, but neither did she after reading some of Hannibal's comments on the photos.

Her other observances? Vincent Kane had more than a

passing interest in the woman who seemed to be Hannibal's apprentice.

Smiling to herself, she wondered how long it would take for Vincent to break away from his dick of a partner and when he'd come to his senses and say something to the apprentice in the shop.

Leaning her elbow on the counter, she looked out of the window at the other building.

While Ronan had never really used the storefront on the ground floor, using that as file storage instead, it would make a kick ass tattoo shop.

Humming along to a song that came up over the speakers, she smiled.

The last photo of the bunch was of the other woman, smiling and looking into the camera. A mirror behind her showed that Vincent was the one taking the photo.

It was labeled, Apprentice Layla Webber.

Maybe it was because she was head over heels in love with Ronan, or maybe it was just her sentimental self, but she was really hoping that they'd have some new neighbors soon.

And she had money that their names were going to be Vincent and Layla.

INKED BY THE DAD BOD

INKED BY THE DAD BOD

It's hard to predict what brings two people together.

Lily and Vincent are two who find themselves drawn together with the inevitable pull of magnetism. Are they a pair of opposites drawn together in a perfect match, or are they too much alike to be together?

Vincent Kane never really considered himself a tattoo artist. He found himself drawn to the craft for its own merits. The artistry was a product of his mind, his building business to his hard work and determination.

After a few years as a partner in their current shop, Vincent finds himself disillusioned by his partner and inextricably drawn to his partner's apprentice. How will he straighten the tangle he's made of his life? Especially when he can't seem to keep his thoughts off of his partner's gorgeous apprentice.

Lily Weber found a position as an apprentice at Ink Envy, but she's worried that she's out of her element. Tattoo artist 'Hannibal' Baldwin is talented, but he also makes her skin crawl.

He doesn't seem to be as interested in helping her develop the skills of her hands as he wants to get his hands on her. If only he was like this partner, Vincent. Lily can't keep her mind off of the other artist who headlines the shop. He features in her dreams both night and day.

Life seems to throw them together over and over, but there's a tall and oh-so-handsy obstacle between them. What will it take for Vincent and Lily to find that they can create more than art? They could create a lifetime of beauty... together?

Lily may find herself Inked by the Dad Bod.

CHAPTER ONE

LILY

Lily Weber had made some horrible decisions in her life and yet she was still alive. She held onto that thought in a moment like this.

"Babe!" Her mentor and boss, 'Hannibal' Bill Baldwin barked at her from the front of the tattoo shop. "Get me some wipes!"

She stood up from her seat at the front desk and grabbed a new package of wet wipes from the cupboard that she stocked herself. She tucked the package under her arm as she snapped a latex glove on both of her hands.

"Babe!"

"I'm here. One sec." She pushed open the door to Hannibal's personal space and try as she might, she couldn't quite ignore the buxom blonde who was splayed out in the tattoo chair. Bambi, and yes, that was the name on her license, had come in for nipple piercings, and yet she was butt naked and flushed from head to toe.

The room stank of sex and when Lily reached her hand out, holding the package of wipes in her hand, she studiously kept her gaze away from her boss.

"Here you go, Bill."

He huffed, and then the package of wipes went flying from her hand.

"I don't want to wipe up. That's your job, babe. Not mine."

With her lips pressed together in a thin line, Lily turned back to Bill's client and saw her move away from the chair.

With the woman bare in the tattoo chair, Lilly had expected there to be a good deal of sweat like some people left on gym equipment.

Instead, the milky trail on the seat looked like something completely different.

Lily was a few minutes away from losing the granola bar she'd managed to gobble down during her five-minute lunch an hour ago.

As she struggled to wipe off the chair, she heard Hannibal laughing with his customer.

"I think you should come in next week, honey. We need to take a look at these babies and make sure that you've still got all of your... sensation."

Her breathy laugh made Lily gag. She barely covered her mouth with the back of her hand.

"Hey, babe!" The tone of his voice made it clear that Bill was barking at her.

Lily tensed, teeth clenched, and a muscle ticked in her jaw.

"Make my baby an appointment for *aftercare*."

Oh. My. God.

His baby, as he put it, was gushing with effusive words

that only meant that she had no idea who she was dealing with.

Being Hannibal's apprentice had been eye opening in a number of ways.

She had been hoping for a mentor who was going to teach her. To lead her forward on the path to becoming a tattoo artist.

Instead she got to wipe up his... sweat, prepare his transfers, inks, and all the other bits and bobs he needed to create his art. And to top it off, when he got horny or drunk, which was pretty much every day, she had to find creative and sometimes all too physical ways of keeping his hands off of her.

Lily made quick work of wiping down the chair because she didn't want to spend an extra second in his room.

It was clean. She saw to that, but whenever he was in his room, his *special* combination of his cloying cologne and self-importance made it nearly impossible to breathe in the space that took up over a third of the interior space of Ink Envy.

Try as she might, Lily had no idea what she was learning from him besides the way to be a total douche and toot your own horn.

She washed her hands in the bathroom and scrubbed hard enough to make her hands raw and red. Whatever Hannibal and his lady friend had, she didn't want.

If he says 'babe' one more time, I'm going to treat him like the pig he is.

When she finished, she sucked up what little she had left of her professionalism and made her way toward the receptionist's desk, where Bambi was waiting to schedule her appointment.

Pushing through the retro curtain of beads that had more of an Age of Aquarius vibe to it than a topflight tattoo shop, she had to remind herself that she was just an apprentice.

Something Bill loved to remind her of if she ever opened her mouth to offer up a suggestion. Any suggestion.

As soon as the waist length strands of beads were safely behind her, the Barbie-like smile on her lips faltered a little.

Bambi Nelson was already heading toward the front door with an overly exaggerated sway to her burlesque worthy hips.

She cleared her throat as she stopped just shy of the doors. "Are you... going to help me?"

Lily turned to the desk and her mouth went dry.

In her place, Bill's partner, Vincent Kane was manning the desk.

He turned to look at the door so she couldn't see his expression, but that was kind of a good thing.

She really didn't want to see Vincent fawning over Bambi.

Her gut really couldn't take it.

"Excuse me? Mister..."

"You can push the door open. It swings just fine."

"But," she gave him a breathy whisper, "what if it's heavy?"

He turned his head and that's when she caught his gaze with her own.

Lily couldn't help her reaction.

It happened every time she felt Vincent's eyes on her.

Her skin tinged. Every damn inch of her skin.

Her face heated. Forehead. Cheeks.

Oh, and the skin across her chest, too.

She fought the urge to touch her fingers there and see if she could feel it through touch.

Lily certainly felt it in a few places that she certainly wasn't going to touch in public and certainly not in front of Vincent.

But while she was in bed...

"Ah-hem?"

Lily turned back to look at Bambi, who had one shapely hip poked out and a hand splayed over her extremely low-cut neckline.

"Help?" She smiled and batted her eyelashes. "With the door?"

Lily lifted her chin and smiled like she used to when she worked at her cashier jobs as a teen.

Without wasting another precious moment of her time, she walked across the room and up to the gorgeous woman who'd just orgasmed in her mentor's tattoo room and while keeping a few inches of distance between them. She pushed the door open and held it.

If looks could kill, Bambi was ready to drip acid out of her mouth. "I don't want you, you little bitch." She'd hissed the words out through pearly white teeth and a super model smile.

"Thank goodness for that." Lily breathed out her words as a whisper and then raised the volume of her voice. "You have a nice day."

Bambi turned back with a saccharine sweet smile, but Lily didn't look.

She really hoped that Vincent wasn't buying Bambi's act. If he was, she didn't want to see it happen.

"Lily?"

Vincent's voice slid down her spine like a lover's touch. She couldn't help how her nipples tightened as the sensations worked their way through her body.

She barely held back a whimper.

"If she's going to stand there for whatever reason, go ahead and let the door close. We pay enough for air conditioning without letting it all bleed out the door."

Lily's smile was suddenly genuine.

"Okay."

With a shrug, she turned around and let the door swing shut.

"Hey."

She didn't let Bambi's startled shriek bother her. Lily walked back to the reception desk and stepped behind it to look at the appointment program.

It was still open to Bambi's aftercare appointment.

Lily couldn't help but snort a little as she read that heading.

She caught sight of Vincent in the reflection on the monitor screen. He gave her a little side-eye look as she quickly went over the fields that he'd entered in.

"I saw you go into the bathroom, so I thought I could key in her next session with Bill."

She smiled as she tapped the SCHEDULE button on the screen. "Thanks, you did great."

"I have you to thank for that."

What?

Lily looked toward him and saw his shoulder first. He was standing close enough that she could touch him if she leaned in his direction.

"You don't have to thank me." She closed out the appointment program and turned, letting her hip lean against the edge of the desk. "I was glad to help with the program. It was something like what they used at the spa that I worked for."

"You were working a lot of jobs before you came to work here."

She lifted her gaze to meet his and tried not to look star struck. Vincent Kane was everything she'd wanted in a mentor.

And a lover.

But she didn't have a chance at either.

Unlike Bill, Vincent had morals. That was part of the

reason why she liked him so damn much and the reason why nothing would ever happen.

She barely avoided laughing at her own thoughts by pressing her lips tightly together.

There was no way that Vincent Kane was attracted to her.

He could have his pick of women and given Bambi's petulant pout, she'd tried to rope him in, and Vincent had turned her down.

Good.

Lily reasoned that if she couldn't have him, she didn't want him with a woman she couldn't stand. Especially someone who'd just done... whatever she'd done with Bill.

"What's with that smile, Lil?"

Lil.

Oh the way he said her name.

Yeah, she was done for.

Tingly?

Check.

Aroused?

Check.

Wet?

Hell yes.

"Smile?"

Cheesy much?

She had no 'game' when it came to flirting. She was just too damn awkward to do much more than look silly.

It didn't mean that she could stop herself though.

"Yeah, your smile." He leaned against the desk and put his hand down on the desktop, his fingers splayed and tented on the hard glass top. "You look like you just won something, and you don't want to split the prize with me."

That got an immediate and possibly stupid reaction from her, but again, she had no game.

"What? With you I would. I mean..." She tried to wave off her own flustered feelings. "Well, I would. I just wouldn't share it with-"

The door to the employee bathroom slammed open with the sound of the toilet still flushing in the background.

Bill turned in their direction and gave them a sneering grin as he wiped his hands on his pants.

"Hey, did Bambi leave already?"

Lily was a little stunned and a little...

"We made her an appointment to come back and then... I guess she left."

Lily wasn't sure, but she thought she heard a tinge of humor in Vincent's voice.

For good measure, she looked back toward the door and miracle of miracles, Bambi was gone.

"Well, she'll be back."

Lily turned back to Bill, who was smiling like-

No, she didn't want to know why he was smiling. It had to be gross.

Bill always was.

"So, Layla-"

"It's Lily."

Lily looked between the two men like she was sitting at Wimbledon Stadium.

Bill looked confused at the correction.

So was she, but she was used to Bill calling her by different names. Layla. Wendy. Missy. Callie. She'd stopped counting at twelve because she didn't want to get to thirteen, but there had been more than that. Many more than that.

Still, Vincent knew her name.

And hearing it growled in his deep, resonant voice?

It didn't help Lily fight off her unfortunate attraction to the artist.

As if anything would.

Vincent had dominated her dreams day and night since she'd met him the day she came into the Ink Envy Studio, hoping to become an apprentice.

"Lily?" Bill said her name like it was sour on his tongue. "Really? That's your name?"

She bit into her bottom lip to hold off a caustic retort.

"Whatever." Bill waved it off. "I was just thinking that we should work on your... your-"

"Apprenticeship?" Again, Vincent had no problem speaking his mind. "What have you helped her with these last few months?"

Bill gave him a hard stare and Lily felt her stomach clench. He wasn't a man that liked to be questioned. When she'd asked him questions, he'd shut her down and told her to "Observe more and stop flapping your fucking gums."

It was probably different with Vincent. They were partners. They were both well-known tattoo artists, but up until that moment, she really hadn't seen them talking to each other.

Lily had just seen the men interact with each other in passing.

Bill narrowed his eyes at her and then tilted his head to take a good look at Vincent. His eyes were barely open when he turned back to look at her. "Are you fucking him?"

CHAPTER TWO

VINCENT

There had been many, MANY times that he'd regretted the decision to go into business with Bill Baldwin.

First, when the other man had decided to go by the nickname 'Hannibal' because he didn't want to use the name Buffalo Bill because, "buffaloes are stupid ass cows and I'm Prime Rib." The sentiment made no sense, but the man had media presence and a long line of dedicated customers.

It wasn't until later that Vincent found out his dedicated customers came to see the artist because he threw more dick than ink in his tattoo sessions.

He'd learned that fending off a number of women and men who thought he was the same way.

They were disappointed to find out that he was a tattoo artist and that's what they got from him when they paid for a session.

And lastly?

Hearing Bill, fresh from a fuck session with his latest groupie, accusing his apprentice of sleeping around as if he had any cause to think Lily's sex life was his concern!

"I said," Bill's arms were down at his sides and his hands were clenching and unclenching, "Are you fucking him?"

Vincent was ready to step in, but he had to get a hold of his temper first.

He wanted to plant his fist in Bill's face, right through his nose and into his brainpan.

The fucker had no reason to say anything like that to Lily.

She was a fucking angel around the shop and if she'd shown any interest in Vincent, he would have been hard pressed not to make her his, but the last thing he wanted to do was to tie her to Ink Envy. He hoped that she would finish her apprenticeship in record time so he could get her an introduction to a couple of shops in the city where she wouldn't have to worry about Bill trying to grope her, or worse.

Bill took a step closer, and Vincent took a step in front of Lily.

He put out a hand and planted his fingertips in Bill's chest.

"Don't come any closer to her, Bill. You don't have any reason to talk to her like that."

"No reason?" Bill leaned into his fingers and sneered. "If you're poaching from me, I have every reason to think whatever I like. I could kick your ass for less."

Could?

Yeah, that would be the day.

"Leave her alone, Bill. Lily's done nothing wrong."

"Lily's done nothing wrong..." Bill repeated the words in a childish singsong tone. "Defending her? What did she have to do to get that from you? Suck your-"

Bill stumbled back and Vincent dropped his gaze toward his hands.

Both were now up and between them.

As Bill rubbed at his chest, Vincent realized that he'd pushed the other man back.

"What the fuck, Vin?" Bill paced back and forth like a caged animal. "You going to go to bat over a little bitch? If you want someone to fuck, I've sent you girls. You could have any of them."

"I don't want them!"

Fuck.

Vincent froze after that rather unfortunately worded denial.

The words were true.

He didn't want the women that had thrown themselves at him.

Vincent also knew that the words he'd used made it seem like he wanted Lily.

It was unfortunately true.

He wanted her like his next breath, but he'd worked himself hard to keep that all to himself.

Bill was a special kind of ass, something Vincent didn't know until they'd opened the shop. Somehow, Bill had kept the nastiest part of his personality under wraps until the doors were open and the news was out.

Hannibal Baldwin and Vincent Kane were partners.

And then when things were starting to unravel and Vincent was just about done with Ink Envy, Lily Weber had walked in the door as Bill's apprentice.

All wide-eyed and excited, she was bright and talented. It didn't help that she was achingly beautiful, but it also hurt.

He'd stayed and tried to make it work because the last thing he was going to do was leave Lily alone with Bill.

So far, it seemed like she'd managed to avoid Bill's lechery. Bill's increasingly sour mood and his overt sexual activities in the shop seemed to corroborate Vincent's assumptions.

If Bill had gotten Lily into his... if he'd gotten to her, there would be no escaping his endless replays of his conquest.

Bill didn't just kiss and tell. He liked to use his hands to demonstrate.

Asshole.

And now, Bill had a scent in his nose.

Things were going to be more difficult in the shop for both of them, but Vincent didn't care how hard it was on him if he could keep Lily safe until she got out from under Bill's thumb.

"Well," Vincent saw Bill's lips pulled into a sneer as he looked at Lily and then Vincent in turn, "you trying to poach my apprentice Vin? You know that's the worst kind of asshole behavior, hmm?"

It wasn't nearly as bad as what Bill was doing.

"It's a problem in the world of ink, Bill, but the kind of shit you're doing to Lily could put us square in the center of a lawsuit."

If Vincent thought that would shock his business partner, he was wrong.

"It's only a lawsuit if she's a little bitch and can't get on board with how things around here are."

Vincent reached out his arm and unerringly found Lily's hip, moving her behind him further. "This isn't one of those shops, Bill. I don't want to work with someone who thinks it's okay to put anyone who works here into a situation where they have to decide between their job and their safety."

"You really are a goody-two-shoes, aren't you, Vinny. If you don't want to work with me, that's fine." Bill pointed past his shoulder toward the light coming in through the front windows. "You know where the door is."

Vincent shook his head. "This is half my business, Bill. We have an equal share and because of that I'm telling you that we're not going to operate like this. Lily came here to learn how to be a tattoo artist. You agreed to teach her.

"Either you do what you promised or-"

"You're just pissed that I jumped in on this and you weren't around when she wandered in off the street!

Vincent shook his head. "What are you talking about?"

"She came in looking for an apprenticeship and you were out that day." Bill leaned closer, but he leaned to the side to get a look at Lily. "I told her she'd have to go through me to get to you. Bitch was so desperate to get in your orbit that she gave in.

"Folded like a poker player with a shit hand." Sneering, he stood up and folded his arms across his chest.

"Or maybe she was just so desperate to get into our shop, she grabbed the first dick she saw."

"Shut up, Bill."

Vincent wasn't sure because he couldn't see her, but he swore he felt her shaking behind him.

"What the fuck happened to you, man?" Bill's whole demeanor changed. Instead of sneering and making fun, his expression had changed to more of a deadpan and his tone sounded like he was disappointed.

Behind him, he heard Lily's slightly muffled voice. "Don't. Please."

Bill continued on. "You used to be a badass."

"It's okay," she sounded like she was speaking through clenched teeth. "Don't."

Vincent felt Lily's hands on his back, her fingers grasping his shirt.

Laughing, Bill rocked back on his heels. "Now you're like a whipped pussy. Or maybe she's just dangling her-"

Vincent swung on Bill.

It wasn't planned, but fuck.

Bill wasn't going to disrespect Lily like that.

Vincent was off-balance with Lily holding onto his shirt and while he clipped the asshole's chin, he didn't get a good hit in.

Bill did.

Rather, he put up a hand to block and missed the punch, but when he bumped into Vincent, Vincent fell toward the wall and his fist connected with the granite tile.

"Oh my god, Vincent!"

Lily managed to keep a hold of him as he went down to the floor, ending up awkwardly draped over him.

When she cried out, Vincent froze.

That was when he heard Bill flip out.

"What the fuck, Lily?"

Oh, great, he'd finally learned her name.

"What the fuck?"

Vincent moved to sit up, but as soon as he did, Lily drew in a gasp. She was in pain.

Vincent glared at Bill. "What did you do?"

"I was gonna kick you in the nuts where you deserve it!"

Lily sucked in another breath and Vincent turned away from Bill.

"Get out, man."

"Look..."

Vincent could see Bill pacing a few feet away.

"I didn't mean... I wasn't gonna..."

That's when Vincent got his arm out from under him and pointed at his partner. "Get out. Give her some space."

Bill came to a quick stop, and Vincent could tell by his expression that he was angry. He looked conflicted, too. Vincent just wanted him gone.

Vincent cast a look over at the reception desk. "Bambi's phone number is on the top of the notepad. Why don't you go and see her?"

Bill almost leapt at the suggestion. He crossed behind the desk, ripped the top paper off the notepad and slammed the front door open in his haste to leave, even though his car was in the back of the shop.

Vincent didn't move until the door closed and the room around them was quiet.

"Lily?"

He heard her draw in a breath, and he rubbed his hand down her arm. It killed him that he was finally touching her, and it was because she was in pain.

"Lily? Where are you hurting?"

She shook her head and her hair fell forward, shrouding her face.

He heard her draw in another breath before she spoke.

"Is it bad to say that I think my pride hurts more than my ass?"

"Than your what?"

Yeah, he heard what she said, but he wasn't going to say the word.

Lord knew he thought about her... backside? butt?

Oh, okay, ass.

He thought about it, practically had the slope of her lower back committed to memory and he'd imagined putting his hands all over the rest of it.

Vincent tried to flex his fingers and bit back a groan.

"Your hand! Vincent, let me see it."

He flinched when she reached for him and heaven help him, he had no idea what she thought that was about. He just didn't want her to see him... like that.

To see him hurt.

That's right, his male ego was bruised.

No man wanted to look weak in front of the woman he wanted.

No man.

It was just in his case that he couldn't help it.

"I don't know what you're trying to do, Vincent Kane, but you better show me your hand."

She'd seen him smash his fingers into the hard stone on the wall. She already knew that he was in pain.

He really had no reason beyond his own fucking embarrassment.

Lily leaned closer and wrapped her hands around his wrist. She gave it a good tug to get him to relax and let her have a good look.

So he gave in.

Partly because her scolding tone was kind of hot.

And when she'd leaned against him, he'd felt her breast press against his arm.

She drew his hand into her space and turned it over one way and then the other as she looked it over.

Her hair had fallen back over her shoulder so he could mostly see her face.

The intent look that settled over her features reminded him of when he'd catch her bent over her sketchpad, focused on her art.

Lily wasn't just beautiful, she was a fucking work of art.

"It's broken, you know."

She startled him when she turned to look at him.

He'd been caught gawking at her.

Or at least he thought he had.

She didn't say anything about it, but she did give him a bossy, cautionary look that made him hard as a pipe in his jeans.

"We're going to the Emergency Room," she announced, with one eyebrow curving up into a classical arch that would be at home in a cathedral, "no arguments."

"Yes, ma'am."

He saw her lips tug up into a smile at the corners as they got up off of the floor together.

And they were halfway to the front door when he realized that she still had her hand around his wrist.

It was childish for him to get bent out of shape because he'd rather be holding her hand, but then again, if she tried to hold his hand, he'd be in excruciating pain.

Yeah, his life still sucked, but Lily Weber was touching him.

If he didn't get himself under control, his dick might bust the zipper down the front of his jeans, and then where would he be?

CHAPTER THREE

LILY

When they'd first arrived at the Emergency Room, there had been so much to do.

First things first, she got Vincent a seat and then she went to the reception desk to get the process started. It didn't help that while she was waiting in line to get to the desk, she could see Vincent out of the corner of her vision.

He looked mutinous.

Or at least that's how she described the look on his face.

His lips were pressed into a thin, pale line and the way he filled the plain, hard plastic chair made him look like a grumpy giant king.

The way he sat against the back of the chair; she was more than a little worried that he might snap the thing into pieces.

The man was what her friends back home called thick.

Well, Kelly had spelled it thicc, with two cs.

But Mary argued that thicc, with two cs, was a word for women. Specifically. in regards to thighs.

To which Jennifer said it was equal opportunity for both sexes. They just had to be 'built.'

That's when someone posted a link to the song BRICKHOUSE.

As she moved up a half step toward the desk, Lily took a quick look at Vincent and concluded, again, that he was most certainly THICC.

The rampant blush that flooded her cheeks made her feel silly.

And more than a little overheated.

Sitting in that horribly narrow plastic chair, Vincent's thighs looked so big! His muscles filling out every spare molecule of space in his worn denim jeans.

It was wrong of her to imagine what he'd look like sitting there in a pair of briefs or boxers.

She'd never been all that interested in sculpting, even at art school, but if she had a chance to run her hands over his thighs, she knew she'd lie like a rug and tell him it was for art's sake.

Lily looked up at the ceiling tiles and mentally berated herself.

Ridiculous. You're being ridiculous! He's sitting there with a broken hand and all you're thinking about are his thighs!

As the line moved forward again, she sighed.

It wouldn't do any good to argue with herself, but she'd been doing a lot of that since she'd started her indentured servitude at Ink Envy.

Bill certainly didn't involve her in any significant way in his work, but she had a lot of opportunities to observe Vincent.

Observe?

Cute word, Lily.

Stare at.

Moon over.

Fantasize about.

They all fit how she felt about Vincent.

While Bill might have had a more public presence, it hadn't taken more than a few days to realize that she shouldn't have been so desperate to jump at working for Bill.

Another step forward and she shook her head at herself.

She'd heard the horror stories when she'd visited shops and talked to women at tattoo shows.

When she'd shown up at Ink Envy, she'd been in shock.

Lily had barely opened her portfolio when Bill had floated the idea that he'd be willing to have her as an apprentice.

After hearing how difficult it would be to find a shop and a mentor, she'd grabbed the opportunity and held onto it with both hands.

How was she supposed to know that Bill was a handsy, borderline misogynistic arsehole?

Time and patience, Lily. Time and patience.

Boy, her inside voice was having a field day.

"Miss?"

Lily's head snapped up when she heard the nurse. "Yes?"

The nurse half-stood to get a look at her. Being petite wasn't as cool as people thought it was.

"Name?"

Lily nodded. "Vincent Kane."

The nurse's fingers paused over the keyboard. "Vincent Kane the tattoo guy?"

Lily nodded. "Yes. That's him."

The nurse looked up at her, narrowing her eyes. "I was

thinking you were the patient. You're flushed so red you look like you've got a fever."

The strange question took Lily back. "I'm sorry, what?"

The nurse sank back down into her chair. "Fever, dear." She gestured in a circle around her own face. "You look like you've been rode hard and put up wet."

Lily laughed at that. She'd spent a little time in a rural area of California as a child and at stables riding horses. So the riding idiom made sense.

The sexual connotation only made her blush worse.

Leaning on the counter, braced on her elbow and using a thick medical folder as a shield, the nurse gave her a big grin.

"So all that heat is because of that man you brought in?"

Lily's shoulders shook and the tension that had been pinching between her shoulders eased away.

She let out a breath and answered the nurse. "Kind of."

The nurse dropped her chin and raised a questioning brow.

"Okay, yes." Lily sighed in surrender. "I practically had to drag him in here. I think he broke something in his hand."

"Oh?" The nurse lowered the folder for a minute to take a look before bringing it back up to 'hide' their conversation. "Did he complain?"

"Actually no," Lily grinned, "he just sat in stony silence as we drove here. I think he didn't want to argue because he knew I wasn't going to listen to it."

"So, how long have the two of you been together?"

"If wishes were horses-"

"You've have a whole dang ranch, right?"

Lily nodded.

The nurse handed her a clipboard and a pen. "Take this over and sit next to the big guy. Or better yet, sit on his lap. I'm guessing it's his dominant hand that he hurt, so you'll need to ask him a bunch of questions. Get the information and bring the clipboard back here.

"It's been pretty busy, but I think you can keep his mind off the pain, if he's lucky."

Lily took the clipboard and walked through the rows of chairs in the waiting room.

For the first half a dozen steps she had to look down to avoid stretched out legs, canes and walkers, but when she looked up from the floor before her, she saw Vincent watching her.

She swallowed hard to clear the knot out of her throat and looked at the only empty seat in the area, right next to Vincent.

The trouble was, she wasn't going to fit.

Thicc.

The word popped up into her thoughts, and she barely avoided groaning at herself.

She really needed some time, energy, and her battery-operated friend before she lost her mind.

"Here," Vincent leaned to the side to give her more room, "have a seat."

Lily decided it was better to stand.

Even with him perched on the edge of his chair, there would be no way for her to avoid his bulk or heat.

Still, she wasn't going to say that. She didn't want him to think she was complaining. "My... my butt still hurts."

"Butt?" There was a moment of humor in his expression, but it faded quickly. "Is that where he kicked you?"

She gave him a one-shouldered shrug. "It's more the bottom of my butt and the top of my thigh. Sitting in your SUV was fine because the cushions were soft. Sitting on a hard chair?"

He nodded. "It would probably be better to sit on the

floor." He gestured to the seat with his left hand. "There are rounded rivets on the seat. That's not any help. Here."

He placed his hand on his left thigh.

"Sit here. There's no other chairs in the room."

Oh, she should have argued and found some other solution, but Lily realized that while she was a grown woman, she had every right to put herself in a situation that was likely to be a big mess.

So she sat down on Vincent's thigh.

"Okay," she focused her gaze on the intake form on the clipboard, "I'm going to need some information..."

CHAPTER FOUR

VINCENT

Vincent found himself somehow grumpier after he'd been given painkillers.

It was his own damn fault, but that didn't mean it was any easier to accept.

"Mister Kane?"

Vincent lifted his gaze to look at the doctor. "Sorry, I'm distracted."

The silver-haired doctor gave him a smile. "Does it have something to do with the lovely young woman in the waiting room?"

The smile that had been lifting the corners of his mouth fell away.

"What about Lily?"

The doctor's eyes widened, and he held up his hands, one with a pen held between his fingers and the other gripping a medical folder. "I'm sorry," he cleared his throat, "I didn't mean to offend."

"I'm not offended." Vincent turned his head in one direction and then the other, cracking it to relieve the pressure that pinched in his neck. "I'm just protective of her."

Vincent lifted his hand, which was swollen and angry looking.

"I let my guard down a little today and ended up punching my business partner for getting rough with her."

The doctor's expression darkened. "I hope he's learned his lesson."

Vincent shrugged his shoulder. "He's a little dense, but I'll make sure he knows to keep his hands off of her from now on."

With his face losing some of its own tension, the doctor opened the medical file and pulled out an x-ray.

"Speaking of hands," he smiled at his own questionable humor, "let's take a look at what we have here."

When he reached the wall, the doctor flicked a switch and the rectangular frame affixed to the wall blinked and then flooded with bright light.

The doctor clipped the x-ray to the frame and pointed out a few places on the x-ray, but to Vincent he sounded like the teacher on the old Peanuts cartoons.

Wha-wa-wa-wha-wa...

"Is there anything broken?"

The doctor went silent, his lips pressing together into a thin pale line. "Please don't take this the wrong way, Mister Kane, but you seem to be a little distracted. No, nothing broken, but you've done an outstanding job of damaging the soft tissue in your hand."

Before Vincent could mutter an apology, the older man smiled. "I'd be impatient to get out of here if I had someone like your Lily waiting for me."

Your Lily.

Vincent's mind echoed the words in his skull, and it quickly changed to '*My Lily.*'

If wishes were horses...

"So I'm going to have the nurse come in and bandage your hand. Before you leave, see the nurse at the reception desk. She'll print out the care instructions for you. Do you have an orthopedic doctor of your own?"

Vincent managed to shake his head to answer. "I can find one."

Reaching into the pocket of his coat, the doctor pulled out a card and wrote something on the back. When he was done, he turned it around so Vincent could see that it was a name and phone number.

"This is a friend of mine. He's the best I know. He'll make sure you're well taken care of. And when you're back to full fighting strength, let me know." He turned the card back over to the front where the ER doctor's information was printed. "I've been meaning to call in and make an appointment at Ink Envy."

"You know who I am?"

The doctor unbuttoned his cuff and pushed it up his forearm an inch or two. The ink he revealed was black and grey realism. Vincent couldn't tell exactly what it was, but the ink work was meticulous.

When Vincent looked up, the doctor smiled. "I've been following you for a while now." He started to push his cuff back into place. "So, take care of that hand, Mister Kane. I'll be looking forward to a call from you."

A soft knock at the door turned Vincent's head.

Of the two women who were standing in the door, Vincent only had eyes for one.

Lily's eyes were round, wider than he'd seen them.

The emotion he saw in her eyes made him regret that he'd asked her to stay out in the waiting room.

"Vincent?"

Her voice sounded so small, soft... almost breathless.

"Are you... Is it..."

He reached out with his left hand and coaxed her forward with his fingers. "Come here."

The nurse walked in after Lily pushed into the room, smiling in her dark blue scrubs.

Gesturing at Lily, she addressed him and the doctor. "I've already given Miss Weber the care instructions and the information on a store with the supplies she'll need to help him care for his injury."

Vincent looked down as Lily took his hand in her own.

"I hope that I didn't overstep."

He looked up into her eyes, lifting his brows in a silent question.

"You're going to need to change your bandage out from time to time, and I couldn't see how you would do it on your own."

He opened his mouth to tell her that she didn't have to take care of him, but behind her, two more nurses stood in the doorway of the exam room, listening intently to the exchange.

They both shook their heads almost frantically and he took their silent, albeit unasked for advice.

"You sure you can handle a grump like me, Lily? I've been told I can be scary before my coffee."

She recoiled a little, her incredibly delicate hand still holding onto his uninjured hand. "Who told you I said that?"

"I may be an ass from time to time, Lily. But I also overheard you on the phone with one of your friends."

She lowered her head as if she was going to hide from him.

"Hey." He gave her hand a squeeze and she looked up at him again. "Don't hide from me. I know what a grump I am on the best of days. If you want to help me with this, I'd be grateful to you for the help."

Vincent felt a little shiver roll through her hand, and he lowered his gaze down for a moment.

He didn't think she knew it, he certainly hadn't until he'd seen it for himself.

Their hands had shifted while they'd been talking. He was holding her hand now, his thumb rubbing softly across her palm in a soothing gesture.

"That," the doctor's voice turned Vincent's attention back in his direction, "and you're not allowed to drive with the meds we gave you."

"That's even more of a reason to accept help from Lily."

Vincent narrowed his eyes on the curvy blonde nurse and saw the way she bit into her bottom lip even as she was smiling.

He had a feeling that the hospital staff was doing its best impression of a dating service and in some ways, he was more than okay with the assist.

He just didn't want Lily to be pressured into anything.

They still barely knew each other.

"Hey."

He looked back at Lily and noticed that it was her hand and her tender touch that was soothing him.

"Don't second guess it." She smiled and her eyes sparkled even with the loud fluorescent lights filling the room. "With Bill going to spend time with his client and your hand hurting, it's not like I have anything to do at the shop. I can switch the phones to ring through to another number so I can help you."

Inspiration hit him like a sledgehammer.

"And while you're helping me, we can work on building your ink skills."

One moment he was carefully examining her face and then in the next he had his good arm wrapped around her willowy body and his face all but buried in the dark waves of her hair.

Fuck.

His mind short-circuited a little as the blood in his body shot toward his dick.

He had no idea what scent she had in her hair, but he knew one thing for sure, he wasn't going to be able to get enough of it.

If he wasn't careful, he'd end up leaning in to take a sniff of her hair like some kind of creep.

Worse?

His injured hand ached even more, wanting to touch her.

Vincent knew he needed to get home. If he managed to get some time to himself, he was sure he could use his left hand to work out some of his frustration.

It was one thing to have dreams about someone you work with, it was another thing entirely to have her in his home.

She'd already been in every room half a dozen or more times in the last few weeks.

He wasn't just an artist with his hands and ink, he had a very vivid imagination, too.

Vincent was damn sure that he could draw her likeness from head to toe in exacting detail from memory.

Something he'd never tell Lily because he was afraid he'd scare her.

But it was what he'd had at his disposal when he was struggling with his attraction to the younger woman.

"Are you ready?"

Vincent turned and refocused his eyes on Lily. "Ready? I'm ready to get out of here."

Lily tried to step back, but he kept a hold on her hand.

It was probably a selfish gesture, but he couldn't seem to help himself.

Not with her.

It didn't hurt that the hospital staff looked like they might break out into applause if he stayed much longer.

Hell, he'd be tempted to join them and that made him smile.

"Looks like that pain medication is helping," she smiled at him when he turned his head in her direction. "You look a lot better."

"I *feel* a lot better."

She walked down the hall with a lightness in her step and her hand still holding on to his.

Yeah, he felt a whole lot better.

It was all because of Lily.

CHAPTER FIVE

LILY

Waiting for Vincent in the Emergency Room waiting area was bad enough. She had time to think and over think everything that had happened that day.

Had she done something wrong?

What if Vincent's hand was broken?

What if he...

No. She wasn't going to let her thoughts go there.

It was going to be okay.

She was going to be there to make it okay.

She'd stood up.

She'd sat down.

She'd paced to the bathroom door, only to turn back around and go back to her seat.

Then the vending machine.

God bless the vending machine.

Thirty-two choices of items to buy. Sodas. *Healthy* drinks. Chips. Cookies. Candy bars. There was even gum.

Not that she chewed gum.

It hurt her jaw.

But it was nice to stare at it.

It wasn't until she made her second trip to the machine that she actually bought something.

A candy bar.

And she'd peeled the wrapper off and eaten the bar and promptly forgotten what she'd even pulled out of the machine.

It had been a terrible godsend when the nurse had come to get her and take her to the exam room where Vincent was.

It was the same nurse who'd taken her arm to steady her when Lily had almost tripped and fallen into the wall and as they walked, the nurse handed her what looked like a ream of papers, telling her that it was Vincent's care instructions.

Lily held the papers tightly, just in case the nurse asked for them back. The last thing she wanted was for someone to take away the papers.

Care instructions meant that he was leaving.

Care instructions meant that he might need her help.

But she wasn't going to let go of the anxiety and worry churning inside of her until she saw him with her own eyes.

Until she saw for herself that-

"Right here. In this room."

Lily stepped inside ahead of the nurse and let out a shaky breath of relief. He didn't have a cast.

The rest of their time in the exam room was mostly a blur. Except for the demonstration from the nurse when she'd put the tight bandages on his hand to keep the swelling down and stabilize his hand.

Lily had video taped that with Vincent's phone. Her

phone had absolutely no bells and whistles. It made calls and sent texts.

Video was a luxury that she didn't need.

"Hey."

She startled out of her memories and looked up at Vincent. "Are you okay?"

He seemed a little startled at the question, but he didn't respond to it.

"If you want to go and sit back in the car, I can finish up in here."

Vincent's smile was mesmerizing. "I think I can handle a trip to the market."

Heat flooded her cheeks. *That's right*, she argued with herself, *he wasn't an invalid*.

"I didn't hurt my feet."

She swallowed, trying to move the lump in her throat.

No, he didn't hurt his feet, but he'd been hurt.

Defending her.

"You had some pretty strong pain meds." She looked at his face, trying to see if he showed any signs of strain. "I'm just following the doctor's orders. He told you to take it easy."

Vincent lifted his bandaged hand. "With this, Lily. He told me not to do anything with this hand. I have a few more body parts than this."

Oh boy, did he!

Even as she told herself to stop, her gaze roamed over the rest of him. From the flannel shirt that stretched around his arm muscles and barrel chest to the dark wash denim jeans that wrapped around his solid hips and thick thighs. It was only when her gaze started back up from the tips of his Doc Martens boots that she realized just how thorough her perusal had been.

Try as she might to ignore it, there was a definite bulge along his thigh.

"Left."

Oh my-

She wanted to swallow the word back down.

Or she wanted the floor to open up and drop her into oblivion.

Neither merciful event happened and she was left struggling with her own ridiculous Freudian slip.

"Ignore that." She pushed the cart forward, hoping to put some distance between them so she could gather her wits about her.

Given the audible and steady tread of Vincent's boots on the linoleum tile beside her, he was easily keeping up with her.

No rest for the wicked, hmm?

Nope, she decided. She was screwed.

"Lily-"

"Please?" Her voice was a little thinner than she'd hoped. "Can we pretend I'm a few drinks in and my head's all messed up?"

"Hey. Hey, now."

She felt his hand on her arm and she came to a rather inelegant stop in the aisle, somewhere between the prepackaged Asian noodle cups and boxes of uncooked pasta.

Lily turned her gaze to meet his, audibly breathing out a sigh of relief when she saw that he wasn't upset.

Damn it. He was smiling!

"Vincent, I-"

"Just flattered the hell out of me." He shook his head. "I don't think it's any secret how I feel around you. Not after you had to share a seat with me in the waiting room."

Her cheeks heated and she tried to relax into the moment.

It wasn't easy, but then again, being around Vincent from day one hadn't been easy.

When he was in the shop, the air around her felt super charged and she was convinced if she touched him, she just might spark and burn up in flames.

"You were the one I wanted to apprentice with." She let the words fly free, too tired of holding them back, to do it any longer. "I knew both of you through your work. I studied image after image when I was looking for a shop to work in, but I was relieved when Bill was the one in the shop the day I came in."

A cart with a squeaky wheel rolled into the aisle and Lily lowered her voice and continued to talk even though there was someone else in the aisle.

If she kept quiet now, she might never get it off of her shoulders.

"I didn't feel anything for Bill."

She swallowed around the knot that was lodged in her throat.

"I know he's talented. He's a really good artist, too. But he's... callus. He's snide. And he's a big man-whore. None of that bothered me because I knew he'd want the help. He had more than his share of female admiration and women more than happy to let him put more than just ink into them when they were in the chair.

"Not me." She drew in a steadying breath as she saw the other customer stop at the far end of the aisle near the organic veggie chips. "I want you to know that. I want you to know that I'm not one of those girls."

His smile had dimmed during her words, but it lifted at the end of her explanation.

"I know, Lily. I know. I've seen you with him and you've

never been more... or rather less than professional around him."

Her smile and her heart lifted at his words. "Oh good."

They shared an easy moment of silence before she had to add on one more reassuring note.

"He kind of gives me the creeps."

That's when Vincent Kane surprised her.

His head tipped back and he laughed.

Laughed so hard that she swore the whole grocery store went quiet.

And while she stood there shaking with her own laughter, she had a tantalizing view of his Adam's apple. His dark sandy-colored beard had always fascinated her. All the men in her family were clean shaven except for her great-uncle Rick, whose mustache was the thing of nightmares when she was a child.

Vincent's full beard had been a fascination for her since she'd seen his picture the first time.

When she'd met him in person, she'd almost reached out to touch it, not because it was scary or anything like that.

No, it was a part of Vincent Kane and goodness gracious... she wanted to touch him.

Touch every part of him.

She wanted to get him home and crawl up into his lap, wrap her arms around his neck, and-

"I'd give everything I have to know what you're thinking about right now."

There was something about Vincent Kane, she decided.

Something about him that took her thoughts hostage, tied them up and held them tight.

And she loved every minute of him.

No, it.

She loved every minute of...

"Come here, Lily. Give me your eyes."

She'd done it again.

She felt like she must have been asleep on her feet and dreaming.

She felt his fingers trace the rise of her cheek and when she met his dark coffee gaze, she forgot how to breathe.

"There she is."

She sighed when he cupped the side of her face with his free hand.

"Come on. Let's go."

His hand moved away from her face and a moment later, he was handing her the straps of her purse.

When they almost reached the end of the empty aisle, she started to turn back. "Our cart. Our supplies."

He took her hand, lacing their fingers together. "There's this thing called delivery, Lily."

"But-"

"As much as I'd love to stand here in the grocery store and watch you daydream, I think I'd rather go home and get a chance to talk to you.

"We'll order in for dinner tonight and we'll worry about tomorrow... tomorrow."

"Tomorrow," she felt heat suffuse through her body from her heart outward, "I like the sound of that."

CHAPTER SIX

VINCENT

He was feeling a little selfish.

Or at least that's what he worried that he was feeling.

Lily had literally promised to help nurse him while his hand was injured, but he knew it wasn't just because she was nice.

She was, but he knew, or rather, he hoped that she was feeling the same way he felt around her.

He'd never been this tied up inside around a woman.

He'd been with women before, both as friends and lovers, but he'd never been *in* love.

And even though he'd known Lily for a short time, he found himself leaning into every minute around her like she was the sun.

Maybe this whole thing that had gone on at work had been just the kick in the pants that he'd needed.

Instead of mooning over her, he had a chance to see where this could go.

He shifted in the passenger seat of his SUV. The seatbelt scratching the side of his neck. "There's a turn coming up. There's a sign for a private road on the right."

Lily turned her head toward him, a quick look at his face. "That's the road?"

"Yeah, that's it."

"Okay." She smiled and tapped the control for the signal. The soft rhythmic tick tick tick of the turn signal calmed him a little. "I'm not used to this part of town."

You will be.

He smiled at his own thoughts and turned to look at her. "It's an older part of town. I think the city planners forgot about it for the most part. There's only a couple of houses on the road and we don't even have a sign marking it."

He pointed out the pole as she turned on the road.

"The sign fell off during a storm a handful of years ago and even though we reported it to the Department of Transportation, they never replaced it."

Vincent watched as she leaned closer to the windshield as she drove down the road. The sun was nearly gone below the horizon from where they were but there was still some ambient light slanting through the leafy canopy of the trees.

"It feels like we're out in the woods."

The soft tone of wonder in her voice touched him. He felt it glide across his skin and as his dick thickened in his pants, he pressed his left hand flat against his thigh.

The instinct to reach out and touch her was a driving need.

Vincent wanted to get home so he could put a little more distance between them.

If she wasn't close enough for him to reach out and touch, he might stand a chance.

"It's the one straight ahead at the end of the road."

He heard the harder edge in his voice and when she spared him a curious, worried look, he tried to explain it away.

"I'm just glad to get home."

Vincent saw her smile, and that eased some of his worry.

"I'm also glad that you're coming home with me."

He heard her soft intake of breath and he held his own while he waited for her reaction.

Lily easily drew his SUV to a stop at the end of the path to his front door.

She put the car in park and turned off the engine.

Once that was done, she turned in her seat so that he could see most of her beautiful face.

And then she smiled.

Not just the soft smile from before, but a brighter smile that lit up the air around them.

"Me too."

Yeah, he was in deep, deep trouble.

And loving every minute of it.

"Let's go inside." He reached out to open the door and stopped short. His right hand was bandaged.

Right.

The reason why she'd come with him in the first place.

"Hold on," she had her seatbelt released in a heartbeat and before he knew what she was planning, Lily Weber drew herself up, bracing her knee on the driver's seat.

Then she reached across his body and tugged on the handle of the door. With another quick move, she pushed it open and damn it.

The way she moved across him was pure torture.

The scent of her skin was another temptation that wound him up inside.

And when she drew back to release his seatbelt, he felt her breast brush against his chest.

When she sat back on her bended leg, she looked up at him with a grin, her teeth nipping into her bottom lip.

The sweet expression didn't do a damn thing to ease the throbbing ache he felt.

Fuck.

She was so damn sweet that he wanted to taste her.

All over.

He ground his back teeth together as his mind produced a rather convincing moan in his imagination.

Vincent knew he was wound tight, but there was one thing he knew for certain. One line he'd never cross.

"Lily."

Her smile deepened and her eyes narrowed a little in reaction.

"I want you to know that I'm not like Bill."

"I know that." She shook her head and waved it off with her delicate hand. "You don't have to tell me."

"No, I need to say this." He felt another uncomfortable wave of anger when he thought of Bill putting his hands on Lily. It didn't matter if it was in lust or anger, Bill had no right to touch her... ever again. "I don't expect anything to happen between us."

She frowned and damn it, he wanted to reach out and smooth the lines that tugged the corners of her mouth down. Since he was still seat belted in, it made things even worse. He would reach out across to touch her face, but his injured hand couldn't handle it.

Not yet.

"I know I want something to happen between us, Lily. That should be obvious after what you've seen."

She blushed at the mention of his constant state of arousal near her.

"But I need you to know that no matter what. Even if I'm buried inside you or one stroke away from... from an orgasm, if you tell me to stop. I'll do it."

The words didn't hurt.

Even the idea of stopping when he was covered in sweat, his balls full and tight, and electricity shooting through his spine would likely kill him when it short-circuited his brain, he'd stop.

He'd stop because she said to.

He'd stop because he could never stand to see pain or disappointment in her eyes and know that he'd put it there.

"I knew that." Lily's tone was even, and she easily met his gaze with her own a moment before she put her hand on his forearm.

He felt that touch all the way down to his toes and other... extremities.

"As easy as it was to know that Bill is a total hound, I've seen who you were from the start. You're the kind of guy who I'd welcome in my arms."

Vincent had already been uncomfortably hard before she'd started to talk. Having the soft, delicate curve of her breast brush against his chest had physically hurt him as his dick shifted in his jeans.

But that wasn't the end of his suffering.

The tip of Lily's tongue swept over her lower lip and seeing the shine that it left on the soft expanse of skin, he knew that he was in a special circle of hell.

He' just told her that he'd gladly stop if she just said the word and now it seemed as though the universe was trying to kill him.

Literally.

His chest ached and his dick, well...

The hand that she'd laid gently on his forearm gave him a squeeze, and every nerve ending in his body was alive with wanting.

"Just so you know," her smile broadened as she lifted her hand from his arm and slipped under it to release his seatbelt, "You're not just 'the kind of guy' I'd want."

He swallowed and waited to hear what more she had to say.

Maybe it was just that he was the kind of masochist that welcomed the sting of a tattoo needle in his skin, or maybe he was just that far gone when it came to the gorgeous woman sitting in the driver's seat of his SUV.

When she spoke, he was fixated on her and only her.

"You should know that you're exactly the man I want, Vincent."

He was sure then that he'd somehow managed to fall headfirst into the luckiest day of his life, but just in case, he reached out with his left hand and took hold of her hand.

Lifting it to his lips, he pressed a gentle kiss to the back of her hand, keeping his gaze firmly fixed on her face.

"Let's go inside," he smiled at her somewhat dreamy expression, "together."

CHAPTER SEVEN

LILY

Walking into Vincent's house was kind of a surreal moment.

Up until the moment that she stepped through the front doorframe, she hadn't really considered what his house would look like.

For her, Vincent's natural habitat was the tattoo shop.

He lived and breathed there in her imagination.

"Taking it all in?"

His voice was soft in her ear, but the sensations it created moved all over her body.

"I... I just never really thought about your house."

"It's a bit much for me, but it's been passed down through a few generations. I've never thought of letting it go."

"And you shouldn't."

She meant it.

It looked like it predated most of the buildings in the city, late nineteenth century at least.

Vincent hadn't moved from behind her yet and Lily was beginning to wonder if she was feeling the heat radiating from his body or if it was just her imagination that had her feeling like he was less than an inch away and it was his body heat at her back?

"The house dates back to when Center City was just beginning. For acres around, this was farmland and the three houses in this area were built on the same property back then. This was the original and the other two were built for the sons of the farmer."

She turned her head to look at him and her shoulder bumped into his chest.

Goodness.

He was so close.

Before, when they'd been in the car and then in the Emergency Room waiting area, she'd been this close to him, but she'd been focused on other things. Not just the feeling of his hard thighs and the beginnings of a truly epic erection under her, but struggling to fill out the admitting paperwork for his injury.

But that was hours ago and now, this close, she could see him up close, especially his beard, which fascinated her so much.

She had to force her hand to stay at her side when what she really wanted to do was reach up and touch it.

"There you go again." His words were filled with amusement and when she looked up into his gaze, his dark brown eyes were full of warmth. "You disappear inside of your head. I bet it's a beautiful place up here."

The touch of his fingertips against her hair was soothing, but it also aroused her as well.

"You have the most amazing hands." She spoke softly but with conviction. "I've seen you work on your clients and you're both methodical and easy on them as well. I've never seen any of your clients tap out."

He walked around her to look into her eyes straight on. "That's not so odd."

She shook her head. "I've seen a bunch of Bill's clients do it. They start to wince or hiss. Then they flinch. By the time they tap out, I've seen people tense up and suffer through lots of pain."

"Is it that bad?"

Lily hesitated. She didn't want to cause any more of a conflict between the two shop owners.

"I've seen videos from both of you on the website for the shop and YouTube, but he's not exactly gentle all the time.

"Maybe I don't know enough to really make a judgement call, but when his client starts to say that it hurts or shows signs that they're really not dealing well with the pain, he can get a little... crass."

Vincent shook his head and for a moment she tensed, worried that he might not see things the way she did.

Lily bit the inside of her cheek, worried that she'd gone headfirst into a difficult conversation and they hadn't even gone further than the living room.

"I should make you sit." She reached out for him, her hands landing on his chest. "You shouldn't be standing up like this. I'm supposed to be taking care of you, not starting problems."

Lily leaned to the side to look for the closest comfortable chair or a larger seat, but before she could lean far enough to the side to find something, she felt an arm wrap around her body.

Vincent stepped in, trapping her between his barrel chest

and his arm. When she looked up into his gaze, she was surprised to see him smiling at her.

"Does your mind ever take a break, sweetness?"

She blinked up at him, unsure that she'd heard what she thought she'd heard. "Me?"

He rolled his eyes and felt his hand curve around her waist.

"Are you hurting yourself?" She couldn't keep the pointed tone out of her voice. "You need to rest your hand."

"There you go again," his shoulders shook with laughter, "thinking and more thinking. I wonder what it would take to get you to let go a little bit and relax."

She laughed before she could stop herself and couldn't quite manage to clap her hand over her mouth to hide it.

He shook his head. "You can't do it, can you?"

"Relax?" Lily shook her head. "No time."

The arm around her lower back held her tight, and Vincent moved in closer until she could feel the soft exhale of his breath against her cheek.

"There's a lot I don't know about you, Lily. Too much."

She wasn't trying to move away from him, but she was also trying to keep herself from leaning into his heat. Her hands moved until her fingertips almost reached his shoulders. "The point of me being here is to help you."

"And learning about you," the deep vocal timbre of his voice felt like a physical touch, "is something I've been dying to do."

Really?

Could it be that simple?

Drawing in a steadying breath, Lily moved her hands up until her palms skirted over his shoulders and that simple gesture brought her flush against his larger form.

Solid. Strong. Perfect.

"Vincent, I-"

Knock Knock

Lily pulled back, her heart jumping in her chest.

It felt like she'd been caught doing something... naughty?

Or maybe it was just that she hadn't been ready to cross the line that she'd etched into the ground at her feet.

Knock Knock

Lily took a step back and as much as it pained her to admit, when Vincent's arm released her, she missed it keenly.

"I should get that."

"I should get that."

Lily shook her head at the way they'd copied each other, but she moved toward the door first. "I'll get it. You sit down and get some rest."

Vincent didn't move, but she continued on to the door and opened it just after the third set of knocks.

When she opened the front door, all she could do was stare.

Well, stare and mumble a couple of words.

"Ginger Hill."

Inwardly, Lily winced at how stupid she must sound.

Outwardly, her face felt numb, like she'd just had her wisdom teeth pulled... again.

The woman standing on Vincent's doorstep was indeed Ginger Hill. The Queen of Ink. She could do it all.

Lily looked her over from head to toe and was marveled by everything she saw. The Titian haired beauty looked like she could have been a marble statue from the Renaissance period.

Where Lily was on the thinner side, her arms more suited to a ballet dancer, Ginger was a curvy goddess.

Something in Lily's gut twisted and sank. Standing there

next to Ginger, they were so completely different. Like Yin and Yang.

And maybe it was that difference that helped Lily snap out of her thoughts.

That, and she realized that she was being rude.

"I'm sorry, Miss Hill. Please, come in."

Lily stepped back and mostly succeeded in keeping her head up.

Ginger didn't seem the least bit upset at the long wait on the doorstep. She stepped inside and looked at Vincent standing right where Lily had left him.

The man, even with a bulky bandage over his hand and forearm, looked good enough to eat.

Lily turned to look at the wall, hoping that he hadn't seen the flush of heat in her gaze.

Somehow, she was sure he'd seen it, but she wasn't ready to see his reaction. Certainly not with another person in the room.

What she felt developing between them wasn't something she wanted to share with someone else. It would feel almost... voyeuristic. And Lily didn't want to share... whatever this was with anyone else.

Ginger crossed the room with her long, ground eating strides and before Lily could call out for her to be careful, the statuesque artist sat gave Vincent a half-hug and a bit of a laugh.

"I got your voice message when you were in the hospital. That's when I knew it was serious. A voice message?"

Lily tried to hide her smile. Vincent wasn't big on talking when a short, curt text would do.

"I brought you two some food. I couldn't see her dragging your grumpy ass through a grocery store. So I left you a message to tell you that I'd bring over some supplies, but I had a feeling that you didn't check your phone."

Lily almost choked on a cough.

Vincent let out a long sigh. "You know I didn't."

So did Lily.

Lily could tell that Ginger knew Vincent well. Given that he'd messaged her with the news that he was in the Emergency Room, he knew her too.

Standing there, Lily knew that she was being a bit of a voyeur as well and found a way to give them some space.

Walking up to them, she held her hands out. "Would you like me to take that and put it in the kitchen?"

Ginger gave her a knowing look and nodded. "Sure, sugar. I picked it up from Gennaro's." She looked at Vincent and then back at Lily. "Just so he doesn't have to suggest that I'm trying to kill the two of you."

Two of us. Lily smiled easily at her words.

"I knew you wouldn't poison Lily, Ginger. It's me that I'd have to worry about."

Ginger gave over the bag easily enough, but it was the look of cartoon warning that she gave Lily right out in the open. "I know they say poisoning is more of a woman's weapon," she winked, "but with this lummox, I'd take too much pleasure in kicking his ass fair and square."

Vincent sighed and shook his head.

As Lily walked into the kitchen, she heard him grumble.

"I'm glad you came by, Ginger."

CHAPTER EIGHT

VINCENT

The moment that Lily left the room, Vincent felt himself burning under the interrogation-strength light of Ginger's pointed stare.

Before she became the best female inker in the country, she had been a kick-ass police officer.

At moments like this, he wondered if she missed her calling. One narrow-eyed look and he was squirming.

"So," she raised a sharp eyebrow at him, "you finally got your shit together with Lily?"

Vincent reached out to take her by the arm and had to switch to his non-dominant hand, but even though he had more than his share of muscle under his larger frame, it took a strong tug before she moved with him to the couches in the living room.

He settled into the deep cushions and gave his old friend a look of his own. "I told you about that in confidence."

Her shoulders shook with laughter. "You mean that I had to literally twist your arm behind your back to get you to talk?"

"You drive a hard bargain." He couldn't help the deep rumble of discontent in his chest. "I don't have anything more to add than what you know."

Ginger shifted forward, bracing her arms on her knees as she gave him an incredulous look. "She's in your house, Vin."

Vincent opened his mouth and closed it again. He didn't know what he should say with Lily across the way in his kitchen.

With a huff, he pushed off of the back cushion and copied her stance. "I think..." He bit into his lower lip and weighed the options in front of him. What to say. What not to say. "It wasn't like I planned it, but I got hurt today and she's been with me since then."

Ginger's smile pulled at the corners like the Cheshire Cat. "Oh, there's hope for you yet. You can benefit from the Florence Nightingale syndrome."

It sounded interesting and vaguely familiar, but he wasn't sure he could trust Ginger to shoot straight at the moment. "You're making that up, aren't you?"

"Nope. It's a thing. When someone takes care of someone else, usually it's a woman thing, they fall for their patient." Ginger shifted on the couch, leaning on the plush armrest, and moved her hair back over her shoulders. "Do you think you can act like a wounded bird for a week or so? You know, sound a little needy for her attention."

That didn't sit well with him. "I'm not going to fake a thing."

She smiled even wider at him. "That's what she's supposed to say."

"Ginger." He leaned closer to her and lowered his voice. "This isn't easy for me."

"Well, duh." She rolled her eyes. "That's why you need me, Vin. I'm a worldly woman with some feminine wiles that I haven't forgotten hanging around swingin' dicks like you. I can help you navigate the sea of love that you'd likely drown in without me."

He felt a muscle in his jaw tick at the laughter he could see in her eyes. "I think I'll be fine, Ginger. I think I can figure this out without your play by play instructions."

"I dunno, old man." Ginger gave him a pointed look and waggled her eyebrows. "I can give some pretty awesome play by play instructions. You'll have that girl screaming your name before you know it."

"Ginger, stop!"

She clapped her hands together and collapsed back against the cushion. "God, Vin. It's too damn easy to ruffle your feathers."

He tipped his head back and looked up at the ceiling. "Why do I put up with you?"

"Because you love me, you big galoot." She gave the sofa seat beside her a big slap. "And I'm your damn neighbor for at least another year. So you better put up with me."

"I could build a wall," he grumbled under his breath.

"You got that much money sitting around, Vin? If you do, I suggest you spend it but not on some damn wall." Ginger tapped her fingers on the sofa cushion, and he heard the taps like the faint patter of rain on the roof. "I was going to come over and see you tonight before you even texted me about your *white knight* demonstration."

Vincent felt his neck tense up at her jest.

"There's a space opening up beside my shop." She wasn't even looking right at him, but she held her hand up to keep him from talking because she must have known he was going to grumble something back at her.

Ginger had always been good at cutting through his bullshit.

"Just listen, okay?"

When he stayed silent, she fought off a bigger smile as she began to speak again.

"It's the salon next door to my shop. The owner is in her eighties and if it was up to her she'd die with her clippers in her hand, but her staff is aging out and like she's said a few thousand times, she doesn't have it in her to learn 'those newfangled hairstyles.'"

"I thought that was a retro place or something like that."

Ginger giggled. Actually giggled. "It's retro now, but she's been doing the same styles for decades. Most of her clients have walkers or wheelchairs. So there's an ADA ramp from the back parking area into the shop."

"You know I already co-own a shop, right?"

Her eyebrow raised like she was doing her best impression of a judgmental owl. "You co-own a shop with an aberrant human. I don't know how long you can stay there with him."

Her gaze lowered to his hand.

Vincent didn't have to look down to know what she was doing.

Yes. He'd punched Bill over how he treated Lily. As much as he felt for Lily, he knew that Bill's treatment of women in their shop had gotten under his skin long before the punch.

"You don't need to have a psychic read your palm to tell you that he's only going to get worse. It's only a matter of time until he's got the both of you in trouble because of his actions.

"All it's going to take is one woman to get mad and start something."

"I don't like what he does with women in the shop," he tasted bile on the back of his tongue, "I've tried to talk to him about it, but he keeps laughing it off."

Ginger openly stared at him. "What's going on with you, Vincent? We've known each other for years and this... this just isn't like you."

"I... I don't really have an answer for you."

Surprise. That was the look on Ginger's face.

She opened her mouth to speak, but shut it, and then opened it again. "You know the answer, Vin. You do. You just have to let it in your head."

He wanted to say something. To give her some kind of answer, he just-

"And I'm going to go so you can address it."

Vincent drew back a little. "You don't... You don't have to go."

Ginger got up from the couch, but before he could figure out how to get up and follow without his right hand, she'd crossed the rug and tapped his knee. "You stay right there. I don't want to get you hurt."

She continued on and stopped halfway to the door. Lifting her chin toward the kitchen, she called out. "You can come out of the kitchen, Lily."

Lily appeared in the doorway and Vincent had to catch his breath.

She looked damn beautiful in his home.

Lily stepped out of the kitchen and gave him a quick look with a smile before crossing to Ginger. "It was nice meeting you."

Vincent saw the moment that Ginger shocked Lily, good and truly shocked her.

Ginger pulled Lily in for a hug, almost lifting her right off of her feet.

Her hug was tight, and Lily managed a gasp of air before Ginger set her back down and let her go.

Mostly let her go, because Ginger took Lily by the shoulders and gave her a pointed look.

"I'm sure you were keeping yourself busy because I bet the last thing you were trying to do was eavesdrop."

Vincent sat up to say something in Lily's defense, but Ginger gave him a wide-eyed look and shook her head.

"He's going to go all grumpy bear and want to defend you, but it'll take him a minute to process and know that's *not* what I said.

"So, now I can talk, and he can keep his big butt on that couch. I'm next door, which is like saying I'm in Disneyland and y'all are in the Adventure Park, but I'm there if you need anything."

Lily wasn't sure how to handle Ginger, and Vincent didn't blame her. Ginger was larger than life in so many great ways, but she was also a lot for anyone. Especially the first time they were face to face and up close.

"Even if it's a shovel to hit him over the head with."

Vincent saw Lily's jaw drop.

Ginger took a step toward the door and then turned around to look at Lily again before she turned her head and stared at him, straight into his eyes.

"Or help digging a ditch, about six feet down."

She gave him a wink and gave Lily a big grin and a wave before she went to the door and let herself out.

The room went quiet for long moments after the door lock clicked into place.

Then Lily turned to look at him and spoke in almost a whisper. "So... that's Ginger Hill."

He nodded and softly laughed. "That's Ginger."

CHAPTER NINE

LILY

She wasn't sure there was any air left in her lungs after Ginger's hug and her knees were a little wobbly, too.

Vincent's friend, a paragon of tattoo talent, and gorgeous to boot, was his next-door neighbor.

And she certainly had great taste in food, too.

"She's ah... a force of nature."

She relaxed a little when Vincent laughed in reply.

"That's a good way to put it."

He held out his left hand to her and she started moving toward him before she even made a conscious decision.

When she reached his side and took his hand, she didn't let him tug her closer.

He frowned, but didn't argue.

Lily gave his hand a soft squeeze. "Do you want me to put the food away? I put the cold items in the fridge, but she had two warm plates. I'm guessing you told her you were hungry?"

She didn't quite smile when she said it, but she didn't frown either. Lily was just waiting to see what he said.

"I'm a man," he shrugged, "I'm always hungry."

His laughter was infectious and she closed her eyes to absorb the sound and memorize it.

"Are you hungry, Lily?"

Her eyelids fluttered open and she found herself staring into the dark depths of his eyes.

There was just something about Vincent that called to her in ways she'd never experienced before.

Something deep and elemental.

The same place where she felt her artistic inspiration come from. Inside her heart and soul.

"I... I could eat."

She winced, wondering if he could hear the ache she felt being this close to him.

"Well then," he braced his elbow on the thick armrest of the sofa, "let's feed you."

She felt him lose a little bit of his balance. It was to be expected. She'd broken both bones in her forearm when she was in high school and learning to push up or off of something seemed like it should be easy.

Experience showed that it wasn't.

Vincent tried to let go of her hand, but she didn't let him.

"Use me to help you get up."

He tensed up a little at her words and she stopped trying to move into him.

"Vincent, what's wrong?"

He cleared his throat and didn't quite meet her eyes.

"I'm not a small guy, Lily. I probably outweigh you by a hundred pounds or more."

"Huh." Her voice was soft but not tentative. "Okay. And?"

"So," he shrugged, but even then she didn't pull her hand away, "you should let me get up on my own."

"I could, but this is all new for you." She tried to ignore the voice inside her head that said her forward behavior was new to her too, but he didn't need to know that. "Let me help you until you get used to doing things without putting pressure on your hands and fingers."

When he still hesitated, she thought it would help to share a little bit of her own experience. Maybe then he'd listen to her, even just a little.

"I broke both bones in my forearm when I was in high school," she began. "It was during P.E. and I while I could dance, I was basically a klutz in any sport. I missed kicking a ball that was basically stationary in front of me on the grass and ended up falling backwards.

"I put my hands down to break my fall and-"

"Broke your bones."

She drew in a deep breath and sighed it out. "Yes. The school nurse took one look at my Tetris piece of an arm and fainted dead away. I almost fainted too, but the pain made it impossible.

"After I got the cast on I went home and let the pain meds work their magic. They probably had too much magic because when I woke up the next day I'd forgotten that I had a cast on my forearm. I swung my feet down to the floor and lowered my arms to help push me up and out of bed and my wrist didn't bend like I expected it to."

She heard him hiss in sympathy and while she talked, she drew his good arm across her shoulders and wrapped her other arm around his back and to his waist to help him up.

"I ended up on the floor. The only reason my mom knew I was in trouble was because I landed on my tailbone with a CRACK that made it down the hall and into her bedroom."

Lily had him walking and she didn't feel the need to let go of him.

Honestly, she didn't want to let go of him, so she didn't.

"It was crazy for the rest of that week. I had to sleep on my left side because my right arm was useless in the cast and if I laid on my back, my tailbone screamed in pain."

She laughed as they made it to the table in the kitchen.

"Now," she stopped walking and he stopped beside her, "that wasn't so horrifying, was it?"

"Putting my arm around you is not anywhere in the vicinity of horrifying."

Why did he have to say things like that?

It was only too easy to lean into him every time he said something sweet. And no, it wasn't leaning in the physical sense. She just wanted to be near him emotionally as well.

To keep herself on a somewhat even keel, she looked at the table before she lifted her chin to meet his eyes again. "Do you want me to help you into a chair?"

The growl that climbed out of his throat didn't scare her at all.

Instead, it made her smile.

"So that's a no to the help? Or to the chair?"

– BIG 'N BURLY DUO 2 –

VINCENT

If Lily wasn't so gorgeous, he might have been able to grumble and grouch in a way that was much more convincing.

He could normally get men, bigger and taller than he was, to back away with a narrow-eyed stare or a deep-chested growl.

He just couldn't manage to do any of that around Lily.

Not that he wanted her to stay away.

He'd done a good job of keeping her at arm's length until that morning.

And now she had her arm around him.

"I don't think I need a chair."

Vincent saw the way her eyes widened at his words and her lips parted on a breath.

He liked that look on her.

Soft, pliant, delicious.

With her arm still around his back, he turned and put his back to the kitchen counter and that drew her closer to him.

"I think we can handle it like this."

She blinked up at him. "You do, huh?"

"Yeah."

She reached past him and he heard the soft click of the take-out container opening.

"If you want, we can use the table." As much fun as it was to have her leaning against him, he didn't want to make things awkward for her.

She laughed and rolled her eyes as she leaned back. She was holding a fork with a bite of meat and veg on the tines. "I've never fed a guy before, but I think I can handle it."

"I like being your first."

He watched the way his words affected her.

The cool perfection of her skin heated pink across her cheeks and when he opened his mouth, she bit into her bottom lip.

She focused on putting the fork between his lips, her blush darkening as she accomplished the task.

He closed his lips over the fork and as she pulled it back, he started to chew.

Smiling to herself, Lily reached past him and took her own bite of the meal.

He liked the way she looked and the way she moved.

He loved the way she smelled and the way her movements relaxed as they continued to eat together.

After a few minutes he decided it was time to ask and answer a few questions as they continued.

"I'm not making you uncomfortable, am I?"

She shook her head and offered him another bite.

He shook his head and she took the bite herself. That left him free to talk for a bit. "I want you to know that I don't do this kind of thing."

She paused with the fork in her hand and swallowed her bite. "Invite a woman home to feed you?" She shook her head. "Well, I did invite myself along, so that's all on me."

"I'm talking about holding you. Trying my best to flirt with you even though I have no practice. Probably no skill at all. I just want you to know that if I hadn't ended up in the Emergency Room today, Lily, things would have changed between us."

She reached past him and he heard her set down the fork. When she leaned back to look at him, her gaze was steady. "Changed how?"

"Changed in that I'm done hiding how I feel about you."

He saw her brace herself even as her eyes widened a little with a look that he thought was hope.

Vincent wanted it to be hope.

"Ever since you started working at the shop, I started walking a tightrope, Lily. And I'm a big guy. Tightropes aren't my thing."

She licked her bottom lip as if she was chasing a bit of the dressing that was on the veg in the plate. He imagined the taste of it on her lips and he had to fight back a hard rush of arousal.

"I wish I'd been there when you'd come in. I would have talked you out of apprenticing yourself to Bill."

She lowered her chin a little. "You didn't want me to apprentice under you."

He shook his head. "I couldn't have been your mentor, Sweet. I didn't have that kind of self-control." Smiling, he chuckled. "I guess I still don't have any self-control when it comes to you."

"I'd say you have a lot of self-control."

She put another bite in his mouth and he smiled back at her.

And bless that beautiful woman for what she said.

"I was coming dangerously close to embarrassing myself," she explained. "Every time you came into the shop I couldn't help but stare at you. It was an absolute godsend when you'd let me come in and watch you draw in your booth."

"It was difficult for me too," he conceded. "I liked having you there too much for my own good. It wasn't easy drawing when you were there, though."

She set the fork down and picked up a napkin, dabbing at the corner of his mouth and along the edge of his beard. "Oh? Do tell."

He pulled her closer and enjoyed the heat of her body against his. "It's a version of performance anxiety. I don't want to embarrass myself in front of you."

"Embarrass yourself?" She shook her head and the earnestness in her eyes humbled him. "You're an amazing artist, Vincent. I wish I could see inside of your head when you're creating your art."

He cursed himself for hurting his hand. If he had full use of it, he wouldn't have to worry about how to draw her closer.

Then again, he reasoned, if he hadn't hurt his hand, she wouldn't be there with him, in his house.

His house.

Smiling, he leaned closer and whispered next to her ear. "Do you want to see inside my head, Lily? Do you want to know what I'm thinking about when I'm drawing?"

He heard her swallow and then the soft gasping intake of breath through her lips.

And then he felt her place her hands on his chest between them as she leaned in and whispered back. "Absolutely."

CHAPTER TEN

LILY

When Vincent pushed away from the kitchen counter, she was prepared to step away and give him room, but he didn't seem to understand that.

He kept his arm around her back and walked her through the living room and down the main hall.

"I have a habit of drawing things in my head." His voice felt like a tantalizing touch along her skin.

"I do the same thing," she smiled, happy that they shared that habit. "It helps me to clear my thoughts."

They neared a door at the end of the hall and that's when Vincent's hand on her hip drew her to a stop.

Lily looked up at him with a curious gaze and a raised brow. "Second thoughts?" She smiled, trying to put him at ease. "You don't have to show me. You should be resting anyway."

Something changed in his eyes.

They were darker.

More intense.

And they were fixed on her face.

"I finally have you to myself, Lily. The last thing I want to do is rest."

She turned toward him and put her hand on his chest, surprised at how easily she felt his heartbeat thrumming under her touch.

It felt like a high performance engine under the hood of a race car.

The vibrations tickled against her palm and sent those delicious vibrations throughout her body.

Just standing there with him, her hand on his chest and his arm around her waist, felt more intimate than she'd been with any man before.

Breathing the same air with him, standing close to him calmed her, and eased her worries.

She'd been watching his expression for signs of pain, but he hadn't shown that he was struggling or suffering at all.

"Okay," she gave him a little nod, "then show me, Vincent. Show me your art."

The door was partially open and he turned, nudging it open with his elbow. Then he walked her inside.

"This used to be two bedrooms," he explained as he pointed out the half wall and posts that crossed half of the space. "I opened it up because there were some nights when I stayed up drawing until I was ready to drop.

"And some nights when I didn't quite make it to bed, falling asleep on my drawing table."

He leaned in and she felt a kiss touch the top of her head.

"Come and see what I've been working on since you started working at Ink Envy."

They walked over to his drawing table and he steered her so that she was standing in the center.

"Oh, Vincent." She started to reach her hand out toward the table but drew it back, afraid to touch anything laid out before her.

"Don't be afraid, Lily." He stepped behind her and leaned against her back as he whispered into her ear. "They don't bite."

The purring tone that sent shivers through her body hinted that he just might and heaven help her. She had a feeling she'd be more than happy to have him do that to her.

What would that feel like?

His laughter tickled her in a way that didn't make her want to laugh. She wanted to lean into it like a touch.

Vibrations through their skin.

"You're inside your head again, Lily mine. I don't want to lose you in there."

She turned to look at him, afraid that he might be upset that she'd turned inward again instead of looking at what she'd asked to see.

The look in his eyes as he met her gaze was warmth.

There was an ease she felt looking in his eyes and a warmth that bled through everywhere they touched.

"I said before and I'll say it again, I want to see in your head, Lily. Don't think for a minute that I'll be upset if you retreat into that world."

Lily shook her head. "But you brought me in here to see your work and I *want* to see it, I..."

Her apology was lost in his kiss.

A sweet touch of skin on skin.

A lingering brush of heaven.

When he lifted his lips from hers, her eyelids fluttered open and she fixed her eyes on his.

"Vincent..."

"Don't be afraid of me, Lily. I'm not here to judge you. There's nothing you could do that would upset me besides denying the artist inside of you."

She felt like she was breathing in his words. His convictions shone in his eyes.

"There will be time to see inside my head, Lily." He leaned in and kissed the center of her forehead. "A lifetime if you'll give it to me. So I can learn to see inside of your head too. And your soul."

She would happily let him have it all just to feel his lips on hers again.

To feel his lips all over her skin.

For that, she'd give him everything.

And at that moment, *everything* was her attention.

Lily turned and smoothed her hand over the cover of Vincent's portfolio. The cover was leather, smooth with age, but still protected through care.

She lifted the cover and set it gently down on the surface of the table before she looked at the first drawing on the mountain of work he kept.

Her eyes followed the lines of the drawing, curves, heavy and light in weight. Every bit of ink that Vincent had put to the paper. She followed them across the finely milled paper and when she reached the end, she leaned back and saw the image as a whole.

She opened her mouth to speak and couldn't find her voice.

Her gaze passed over the paper again and she realized that what she was looking at was Vincent's view of her.

"I... I'm beautiful."

She shook her head.

"I didn't mean it like that."

"You are beautiful." Vincent's warmth was at her back. His unbandaged hand on her arm. "So damn beautiful, Lily."

Her hands were braced on the table as she stood, hesitating between two choices. Leaning forward to put distance between them or leaning back against him.

She felt him lean closer.

Felt the teasing touch of his lips against the shell of her ear and the way his beard caught on her hair.

It was like she felt him all over her, even though they were both fully dressed.

All over me.

What she wouldn't give to have that happen.

"Keep looking."

She felt his hand on her forearm, a knuckle or fingertip tracing a line down to her wrist.

"Please, Lily. I need you to see what I feel for you."

She couldn't tell him no.

There was just no way she could deny that simple request.

The next drawing was sweet. A portrait from a moment she couldn't remember.

When had he had the time to study her like that?

"You don't know how many times I've watched you." His voice was deep, almost raw in tone. "Your smile warms me from the inside out. I don't know how it's possible, but it is.

"I see you in my dreams. Day and night. I see you, your beauty inside and out."

She kept going and felt her skin grow hot with wanting and heat pooling between her legs. She wanted him there.

She wanted him... everywhere.

"I... I've never seen myself like this, Vincent. I've never dreamed that you would see me this way."

She drew her fingers over the next image as if it would come alive before her.

And then she realized that it was alive.

She was alive.

But she wanted to feel it.

Feel it through every cell of her body.

In the image before her, she saw herself laid out on a bed, her body nude, her legs spread in invitation, her arms raised over her head as she looked at the artist with love filling her eyes.

"Is this what you see, Vincent? Is this," she traced her fingertip along the line of her thigh in the drawing, "what you want?"

He pushed forward, crowding her against the edge of the drawing table.

She was a little too short to have the edge press against the apex of her thighs, her clit, but it was close.

As was the hard press of his erection against her back.

"I've made love to you a thousand ways in my head."

She heard the deep ache in his voice and found that the same ache throbbed inside of herself as well.

"I've imagined my hands on your body, the flush of blood under your skin. I've dreamed of the way you feel against me... around me. And I've ached to hear the sound of your voice when I make you come.

"You consume me, Lily. I know I haven't said any of this to you before, but I can't help the way I feel. Or the way I need you. Today, when he touched you, I lost a little of my sanity in that moment, but I also found clarity, too.

"I know that I can't stay away from you any more than I can consciously stop breathing. I just need to know if you feel the same way or if you could see it in the future. I'm in no rush, Lily. I'm not going to play games either. If there's a hope that you will give me a chance to love you, that's all I need to know."

She heard his words.

She saw the care and skill that he'd devoted to drawing her expressions and her form and knew that he meant them.

This wasn't a passing fancy or a moment of curiosity.

And she understood how he felt, because she felt it too.

Lily turned, wiggling between Vincent's larger body and the hard line of the drawing table. He took a step back to give her room, but she didn't need it or want it.

She used her hands to grab a hold of his shirt and draw him closer, lifting her chin so her gaze could meet him straight on.

"One day soon," she licked her lips to wet them and saw his gaze flicker down to watch, "I'm going to show you my drawings of you, Vincent Kane. And when that happens, you're going to know that there's more than just a hope of something between us.

"I don't just want you, Vincent. I *need* you. I knew as soon as I started work at Ink Envy that I should leave because Bill was never going to be a real mentor to me. He would never spend the kind of time it took to help me develop into the kind of artist I want to be, but I stayed because I wanted to be near you.

"I wanted to be with you."

And before she could think better of it she took hold of her blouse and lifted it over her head before dropping it down toward her feet.

She stood there in her bra and leggings, looking up into his hungry eyes.

"Maybe we should wait," she murmured softly, "you only have one hand."

Before she knew what was happening, he wrapped his good arm around her and lifted her onto his drawing table.

Her breath rushed out of her lungs when her backside hit the surface of the table.

As he drew back he lifted his chin and smiled. "Lean back, brace your hands on the table."

Widening her eyes for a moment, she did what he told her and watched his gaze move over her body from head to toe and back again.

"Beautiful," he breathed, "just perfection."

Lifting his left hand, he found the clasp between her breasts and snapped it open.

Smiling at her with a wolfish grin, Vincent moved closer, between her open knees. "I may have just one hand, sweet Lily, but I have a mouth dying to taste you."

Oh, good lord, she gasped as he leaned in toward her breast, this was actually happening.

CHAPTER ELEVEN

VINCENT

He'd imagined.

He'd fantasized.

And he'd drawn what he thought Lily would look like when she was bare before him, but he'd never realized true beauty until Lily lay on his drawing table bare from head to toe.

He'd managed to take her leggings off with pure luck, or maybe it was desperation.

Either way, he had her right where he wanted her, under him.

His lips paid homage to the pale perfection of her skin, tasting the blush rising to meet him.

Moving over her, hearing her gasp and moan as he brushed against her sex, his shirt and jeans dragging against her softest spots while his breath played over her skin.

Vincent stopped when he came within a few inches of her breasts.

Her skin nearly glowed under the twilight that poured through the window, giving her an almost fairylike appearance.

He cursed his injured hand again when he wanted to splay his hands across her skin. He wanted to cover her breasts with his hands, palm them, play with her rose-colored nipples.

He could only use the one hand.

And use it, he did.

Lifting his free hand, he stroked the rise of her breast, down and over her pearled nipple, only to circle back again.

Lily shifted restlessly and he heard the crumple of paper under her body.

She stilled and shuddered as he traced his finger around her nipple, her hands grasping for something to hold on the table.

Her hands could only find the hard top of the table, and he heard her knuckles bump against it. The hiss from her lips might have had a few meanings, but as his fingers stroked along the tightening bud of her breast, his lips closed over the other.

"Oh..."

Her thighs lifted and squeezed at his sides, pulling him closer.

Vincent smiled at her reaction and then winced a little as her hand found the crown of his head, her fingers grasping at his hair.

"Don't stop there," her voice was tight, "don't you dare stop there."

"I wasn't sure how you'd like it." He turned his cheek and brushed it along her belly, enjoying the way his beard traced over her skin. "I want you to like how it feels to have my mouth on you."

Her fingernails scraped over his scalp as she tried to bring him back to her breast.

He didn't make her wait more than the moment it took for him to smile at her eager reaction.

He wanted to make her happy.

When his mouth closed over her nipple again, his tongue sought out the tight nub in the center and he heard her reaction to the way he dragged it over her sensitive skin.

Another swipe of his tongue and her back arched from the table.

Lily was so damn sensitive.

He fucking loved it.

Loved her.

He drew back as his fingers twisted and pinched at her nipple and he gazed at the evidence of his mouth on her skin.

He'd marked her in a way, but it wouldn't last.

He'd have to leave it again.

Leaning over her breast, he widened his mouth and drew her in, suckling on her as if he was hungry...

Who was he kidding? He was starving for her.

"Oh," her voice softened as he feasted on her, her thighs clenching against his hips, "Wow. How? Is that... Don't-"

He pulled away and looked up at her from his place, squeezed between her thighs. "You want me to stop?"

She shook her head, her dark hair moving around her face almost frantically. "Don't stop. I want more, Vincent."

He saw the wild look in her eyes and needy pout of her lips.

"I want more."

"Whatever you want, Lily. Anything for you."

He switched his mouth to her other breast, frustrated that

he couldn't use his hand on the first. The last thing he wanted to do was leave her without the sensual touch that she needed.

Vincent closed his mouth around her other breast and the way she reacted turned his already hard cock to iron.

The way that she shifted and arched beneath him reminded him of a wild horse trying to free themselves from the saddle.

Except, the way Lily's hands grasped at him, wrapped around his arms, fisted in his hair, she wasn't trying to get him off of her.

She was trying to get him closer.

He was more than fine with that.

Vincent let go of her breast with a soft pop and placed a kiss on her sternum at the center of her chest and then moved on lower with a kiss just above her belly button.

Then below.

"Vincent?"

He heard a tremor of worry in her tone.

"Vincent, wait."

He looked up at her again. This time she was braced on her elbows, her hair forward over her shoulders and curved near her breasts, letting her nipples play a delicious game of hide and seek with his eyes.

"What's wrong, Sweet?"

"Are you," she swallowed and he saw the rise and fall of her chest made her breasts even more prominent in the light, "are you planning to..."

"Planning to put my mouth on you?"

She nodded, but her movements were so slight that he could barely see it.

"I'm planning to put my tongue and fingers in you too, if that's something you want."

Her mouth closed, but her lips didn't compress into a thin line. Instead, they trembled.

Lily didn't speak, but she nodded instead, and her belly trembled with something he hoped was anticipation.

But there was also something in her eyes and expression that told him it might be apprehension.

"Have you ever had someone eat you out, Sweet?"

She hesitated and then shrugged. "It wasn't... all that good."

His eyes widened at her words. "That's a shame, Lily. A cryin' shame."

"You don't have to," she blurted out the words, and her thighs relaxed around his sides. "It's not something I need."

"Lily, my love," he saw the way her own eyes widened at his words, "I think I can change your mind about it. I know that standing here, with your beautiful body nude and needy under me, I swear I can smell your sweet pussy and I'm starving for it.

"Let me show you how it can be when a man wants you as much as I do."

All he was waiting for was a word, or a nod. He needed her to give him some indication that she wanted to give him a chance.

Fuck me.

She licked at her lips, a slow swipe of her tongue across her full lower lip and a quick flick across the top.

And then she nodded.

– BIG 'N BURLY DUO 2 –

LILY

She wasn't sure this was the best decision to make. The last thing she wanted to do was to disappoint him.

Being with him, making love, wasn't something she did lightly.

He'd called her *my love* and it felt like his words had unlocked something inside of her.

She'd already known that she was in love with him. She had been from that first week in the shop. It hadn't taken more than just a few hours observing him, watching him create.

The last thing she wanted to do now was to make him feel like she didn't want him or that she didn't appreciate what he wanted to do to her and-

"Baby."

She closed her eyes and shook her head.

She'd done it again. Let herself fall into her own thoughts.

"Lily, look at me."

Nodding to herself she opened her eyes and met his gaze.

"That's it, Sweet. That's my girl."

The look in his eyes was like warm melted chocolate. The kind that she could lick straight off of her fingers.

"Are you watching me, *Lil?*"

She nodded and saw the sly smile that curved across his lips.

"Good. Because I'm going to watch you come apart on my tongue. I'm going to drink you down like whiskey."

His voice purred in her ears, tickling along her skin.

Lily drew in a breath in preparation, steeling herself for the first touch of his mouth against her.

But she wasn't prepared for what happened.

The first contact of his mouth against her body.

No, not just her body...

Her body *down there*.

She braced herself, ready to have him pull away or give a half-hearted attempt.

What she got was blinding pleasure.

Maybe it was just his skill.

Or maybe Vincent was just really dedicated to blowing her mind.

It didn't matter.

Not when the hot swipe of his tongue and the rough brush of his beard took every nerve ending in her pussy and set them on fire.

Light flared on the edges of her vision and somehow she felt him lift one of her legs.

A quick, blinking look down over her breasts and belly told her that he'd laid it over his shoulder.

With an effort that left her shaking, she lifted her other leg and set it down over his other shoulder.

Oh, goodness.

It pressed him deeper against her and that added contact had her breathing shallow.

The next sweep of his tongue had her seeing the faintest hint of stars in the air.

"Oh, wow."

Elegant in expression, she wasn't, but her brain cells were barely firing. All that cellular electricity had gone south with the blood in her body.

"Is this," she gasped when she felt his tongue push inside, "is this what it's like when a guy gets a blow job?"

Vincent laughed and she felt her body shake with the sensations that it sent through her.

How was laughter so damn sexy?

That was a question for another day because-

"Oh, god yes!"

His mouth was *there*.

His tongue.

His lips.

The brush of his beard.

All of it focused on that little bunch of nerves that none of her other partners had ever found.

Vincent Kane knew just where to touch her.

He knew just what to do to make her climb higher and higher. Searching.

Reaching for that release.

Just when she was ready to cry uncle and beg him to stop because she'd never once come like this before, she felt something thick and warm push inside of her.

Her hips arched off the table and her hand lost hold of his hair. "What? Oh god, what are you doing to me?"

The thickness she felt inside of her channel moved. It turned and twisted. Curled and thrust inside of her.

"Like that, Lil'?" She heard the deep rasp of his voice and felt it tremor along her skin. "Let's give you more and see what happens."

Before she could ask for mercy, he was back at it.

His mouth.

His fingers.

It felt like she couldn't get any reprieve from the rush of sensations, but she didn't want any either. She wanted to go along with him.

She wanted Vincent to show her what she'd been missing.

Lily just wished that she could help him somehow.

"Vincent, I-"

Something happened inside of her.

Something shifted.

Oh goodness, it was his fingers.

They slid along the upper wall and pressed.

She lost the ability to think.

She was sailing, flying up past rainbows and stars.

And Vincent was there, drawing out her unexpected flight.

He kept his fingers inside of her and she felt the muscles along her walls pulling at him, trying to draw him in closer.

Deeper.

He stood up and gave her a satisfied grin even as her body shook and shuddered as her orgasm rolled through her again.

"I think she likes it."

If she'd had the energy, she might have made some kind of silly or snarky comeback, but she didn't have the energy.

She lay there, boneless, on his desk and wondered aloud. "I hope I haven't ruined any of your drawings."

Vincent shook his head and smiled at her as he lifted his hand to his mouth.

He licked the fingers that he'd just had in her body and gave her a wicked grin.

"I'll just have to draw more. Maybe this time with a live model."

How could he be so sweet and sexy at the same time?

Lily lay boneless on his desk and just concentrated on breathing.

He'd made her come and gotten her completely out of her head for once.

And it was only the beginning.

CHAPTER TWELVE

VINCENT

He woke up the next morning, barely feeling the ache in his hand. He'd broken bones before and made do with stuff from over the counter.

So he wasn't concerned about the pain. He'd go and grab something out of the medicine cabinet in a little while.

For the moment, he was completely satisfied to lay in bed with Lily cuddled up against his side.

It turned out that opening up the wall between his bedroom and office had been the best decision he'd made.

Lily had been a little weak in the knees and the exhaustion of the day and their Emergency Room visit had caught up with them. Even though he'd considered taking their relationship further, by the time they'd crawled up onto his bed, they melted into each other and fell asleep.

Now, with the morning light filtering in through the

windows on the other side of the room, he turned on his side and wanted to brush her hair back from her face.

The only problem was that he'd have to use his bandaged hand.

The last thing he wanted was for her to wake up with him, wincing in pain.

"You're thinking so loud," Lily grumbled and lifted her head to pillow it on his shoulder. "Are you okay? Hurting?"

Vincent smiled at her and her satisfied smile. He leaned in to kiss her forehead. "I'm feeling great with you here."

Her eyes opened and he felt the warmth in her early morning gaze. "Sorry," she murmured softly, "I didn't plan to fall asleep like that."

Vincent leaned in to kiss her forehead again, but she tilted her head back and met his lips with her own.

Her kiss teased and taunted him, her hand fisting in his shirt. "Morning."

He was aching suddenly and it wasn't in his hand.

It was inside his jeans.

Vincent knew that he'd been crazy to fall asleep fully dressed, but he wanted to pull her into his arms before she closed her eyes.

Being with her was worth the painful ache. Having her close was everything he'd ever wished for.

"So," she moved her hand down his chest and skirted over his belly until her fingers slipped in through the gap between two of his buttons, "I think I was a horrible guest last night and went to sleep before we could-"

He reached to grasp her hand to stop her, but drew back with a hiss. "Damn it."

Lily scrambled to sit up, backing away from him so she didn't bump him at all. "I'm so sorry, Vincent, I-"

He caught her hand with his left and held her still. "Don't

be sorry. Having you here with me is worth every little twinge."

She shook her head. "I'm not here to hurt you, I just thought, after what happened on your desk..."

He loved the way she blushed so easily. "You don't have to worry about reciprocating anything, Sweet. I mean it when I say I love having you here with me."

"So you don't want me to... or you don't want *us* to-"

"You're thinking out loud now," he grinned at her and saw the surprise in her eyes, "I like that you can, but you should know that I'm holding back just because when we do make love, I want to have the use of both hands."

He watched her shiver at the promise in his words.

"Okay," she breathed the word out on a smile, "if I can't get you out of your pants right now, what can I do to help around here?"

Vincent shook his head. "You're just trying to tease me."

Lily bit into her bottom lip and her eyes flared with heat. "It's your fault." He heard the tease in her voice and smiled. She caught onto that quickly and drew her legs up to her chest as she wagged her finger at him. "You're smiling."

"Yes." He felt a little bit of an ache in his cheeks. His muscles weren't used to the effort. "That's *your* fault, sweetness."

"I'll take the responsibility for you smiling." She sighed with a bright smile of her own. "I'm going to grab my bag and a shower, if that's okay. Then, I'm all yours for work."

She made it to the doorway before he called out to her.

"Just for work?"

Lily turned back, rolling her eyes at him. "Work. Pleasure," she purred out that word and gave him a wink, "whatever you want. I'm yours, Vincent."

When she left the room, he was left forcing air into his lungs.

Lily Weber made him feel gloriously alive and damn it, she made him smile.

Things were changing like lightning in his world, and he could barely believe his luck.

— BIG 'N BURLY DUO 2 —

LILY

It was a crazy whirlwind.

One day she was slogging through her work for Bill and then the next she woke up in Vincent Kane's bed with his arms around her.

Crazy?

Yes!

But she wouldn't change a thing.

Well, she would've kept Vincent from hurting his hand, but the rest?

She'd keep that and relive it over and over.

She kept blushing every time she thought about the way he'd made love to her with his mouth.

"Hey."

Lily felt Vincent's hand on hers and turned to look at him.

"You have this look on your face."

"Can you see me blushing?" She leaned in toward Vincent and smiled as he grinned back at her.

"You look pretty in pink, Sweets." His voice was deeper

and softer. "It reminds me of how you looked all over when I had you on my desk."

She cast a look at the coffee shop she'd parked next to before turning back to look at him. "Are you sure you want coffee? I mean, if you are, I can make you coffee at your place. You have the same espresso machine that we have at Ink Envy."

"There's another reason I wanted you to bring me here." Vincent lifted her hand and brushed a kiss across her knuckles. "Come on in and meet the owner and her husband. I think you'll like them and the shop."

She turned her head to the side and gave him a little suspicious look out of the corner of her eye. "I see a big menu board in there with all kinds of baked goodies on it. There better be some sugar with my name on it in there."

Vincent pulled her close and covered her mouth with his for a hard, hot kiss.

When he leaned back she was tingling all over.

"Whatever you want. I'll get you. And maybe you'll give me some sugar when we get back to the house."

She smiled and nodded. "Whatever you want," she mimicked him, but changed the end, "I'll give it to you. Now, let's get going."

The shop smelled better than she expected. She'd been in a ton of coffee shops, but there was something about the inside of Milk & Honey that made her mouth water.

Well, Vincent maybe had something to do with that, but it was in the air too.

The bell above the door was still jingling when a woman stepped out into the shop from the kitchen. Or at least Lily assumed it was the kitchen because the most amazing smells came out of it.

"Hey, Vincent! You're back!"

Lily was drawn toward the woman, who looked a little older than her.

As Vincent moved closer, she did too.

"Hey, Poppy! Good to see you again. I brought someone to meet you." Vincent put his left hand on her lower back and Lily tried to fight off the shivers that the gesture sent up and down her spine. "This is Lily Weber."

He paused and they looked at each other, smiling.

Vincent continued. "She's... Uh, she's–"

Poppy clapped her hands together and shook with a giddy laugh. "Your woman! So sweet!"

Lily laughed and shook her head. "Are we that obvious?"

Poppy lifted her hand and pinched her fingers together around an imaginary 'inch,' "Just a wee bit. I'm so glad!"

The curvy woman stepped around the counter and stopped short. "Vincent? What happened to your hand?"

Vincent shrugged like it wasn't much. "Bill put his hands on Lily."

Poppy leaned back, her mouth opening into a surprised O. "And you tore him apart, right?" She waved her hand in dismissal. "Well, he deserved it."

Lily shook her head at the ball of energy she'd been introduced to.

And that ball of energy turned toward her. "Lily, hmm? The name fits you perfectly! Delicate and gorgeous!" Poppy moved closer and carefully wrapped them both in a hug. "I have to admit," she whispered with a broad grin, "I'm partial to flower names and you're so sweet. I bet we're going to be great friends."

There was something that Lily was missing.

She turned and looked up at Vincent.

His grin told her that he was enjoying the moment of confusion. "I met Poppy and her husband Ronan when I came to look at the building across the way."

"It's how we met," Poppy whispered like she was telling the most delicious secret. "Ronan had his office across the way and lived upstairs. This was my shop with my rooms upstairs and I had a little trouble with a guy I dated and one night..." She shuddered. "Well, let's just say he came to my rescue. Now we live upstairs here and he runs his PI business out of here so we can work together, not that he ever used the office across the way."

"Office?" Lily looked at Vincent, narrowing her eyes. "What... is that why you brought me here?"

There was something almost boyish about the smile that Vincent cast in her direction.

"When Ronan moved in here," Vincent reached his arm around her waist and stepped in closer, "I came to look at the space. It's not as big as Ink Envy downstairs if I just use the storefront, but if we expanded things into the rest of the ground floor, there would be room enough for two artists."

Lily swallowed at the lump she felt lodged in her throat.

She wasn't sure if she was reading too much into things, but he'd said 'we' when he talked about expanding the store front and *two* artists, not just one.

Lily opened her mouth to speak, but she didn't have the voice to ask the question her heart wanted to ask.

Vincent smiled at her and moved closer to her until they were almost pressed against each other.

"I want you to know that I was thinking about you then. I'm still thinking about you, Lily. You've got incredible skills as an artist. While Bill hasn't helped you, I'm determined to make sure that you get that training. And when you're ready, if you want to work with me, I'll have the space for you at-"

She kissed him.

No.

It was more than that.

She gave him a promise.

When she broke away she looked up at him, both of them short of breath and smiling. "If? Are you kidding me? That's a yes!"

A soft sniffle turned both of their heads toward Poppy. The coffee shop owner was dabbing at her eyes with the edge of her apron. "Y'all are so sweet! It's like you proposed right here in my shop."

Lily opened her mouth to correct Poppy.

It wasn't a proposal.

It was just...

Well...

Vincent tugged her closer and whispered in her ear. "I'm in this forever, Lily. Shop? Marriage? Kids? Everything."

Lily was suddenly shocked and parched.

"You two sit," Poppy shushed them toward a table, "I'll bring out some treats and two of my best coffee creations. I think this has been a bit of a shock for Lily. You should get her to sit down and we'll get something sweet and *delish* into her and then you can show her the space. Ronan should be back in about a half an hour, so he can take you over to look. If you're not sick of us by then, we'd love to have the two of you stay for dinner."

As Poppy disappeared into the kitchen to grab some pastries, Lily sat down at a table beside Vincent and shook her head. "Wow."

Vincent's smile was tempered with a bit of worry. "Too much, too fast?"

Lily reached out and set her hand on his hand, enjoying the heat of his skin. "I feel like we're just catching up on lost time."

The look he gave her in return had her heart pounding in her chest and arousal pulsing through her veins.

"I'm going to make every minute we're together worth it," he vowed.

"You already have," she drew in another deep shuddering breath, "you already have."

CHAPTER THIRTEEN

VINCENT

Vincent heard a soft knock at the door.

Lily looked up from the draft table where she was working and set her pencil down. "Are we expecting something?"

He looked down at the watch on his arm and smiled. "I'll get it."

Lily, already halfway out of the chair, gave him a curious, narrowed-eye look.

She was out of the chair before he could stop her, but he caught her around her waist and pulled her in for a quick, hard kiss.

"Sit." He nudged her back to the table.

"Woof." She gave him a sour look, but there was a spark in her eyes that told him she was just playing.

Vincent started for the door, turning to gesture at the table again. "Work on finishing that drawing, I want to get it printed out on transfer paper."

He walked away, smiling as she grumbled under her breath.

"Yes, sir."

Vincent bit back a groan. He didn't think she meant it the way his dick heard it, but he was fairly sure that his thoughts were a little dirty when it came to his...

No, she was his.

His Lily.

Just before he reached the door, he looked down at his right hand and the temporary brace that the doctor had put on for him.

He was resting his hand as much as he could because he wanted to heal as fast as humanly possible. Intimacy with Lily was a dream. She was responsive and passionate and even though she wasn't practiced, she was enthusiastic and he encouraged her in so many ways.

When he opened the door he had a broad smile for the courier.

The man in the Pullman brown uniform on the porch gave him a curious stare. "Mister Kane?"

"Is that my package?"

The courier turned his handheld device around. "Signature, sir."

Vincent lifted his right arm and huffed.

Before he could pull his thoughts together, Lily appeared at his side.

"Here, I can sign that." Lily stepped out onto the porch in her bare feet and reached for the device.

Vincent saw the way that the courier stared at her and Vincent had to draw in a deep, full-chested breath to keep himself quiet.

Her loose open necked top gave him a teasing look at her sports bra underneath and when Lily held out the device to the courier, he didn't immediately take it.

Vincent turned his head to look and saw the man staring at Lily with appreciation and more than a hint of arousal in his eyes.

He lifted his right hand to take the device and shove it at the man, but Lily beat him to the punch.

"Here you go. Thanks for bringing the package." She walked past the man, putting the device heavily in his hand. She picked the package up off of the railing and headed back inside. "Thanks again!"

Vincent smiled at her overly-chipper tone and for a moment fought off his urge to offer up a single-fingered gesture to the courier, but he held off.

He walked inside and followed Lily into their bedroom.

She was wearing a pair of shorts folded over at the waist, so it rode on the crest of her hips.

Walking away, she gave him the sweetest view of her backside.

Just before she turned into the open doorway, he heard her laugh.

"Are you staring?"

"I'm weak when it comes to you, Sweets. Of course I'm staring. I can't wait until I can get both of my hands on your ass."

She sighed, but the tone was sweet with humor. "You're so lucky I think you're hot."

Yeah, if he wasn't already hard, he would have been after that teasing comment.

Lily put the package on the table and turned to look at him. "So, what did you order?"

He reached out with his left hand and gripped her waist before stepping closer to her.

"You make it hard to keep myself focused on business, babe."

She laughed and smoothed her hand down his left arm. "Silly. Seriously though, what's in the box?"

He started to reach into his pocket for his keychain with a pocketknife and stopped, grinding his back teeth together.

Lily was already there with a pair of scissors held open to use one side as a blade. "Can I?"

He gestured her for her to go ahead and she did, carefully cutting through the packing tape.

As she opened the top flaps of the box with one hand, she set aside the scissors with the other and reached for the packing.

"It's something I wanted to have you test for me." He watched as she pulled out the first item, wrapped in a piece of plain muslin fabric. "Don't worry, Sweets. It's not human."

She started to unwind the fabric. "Not human? What do you mean- Oh!"

Lily almost dropped the arm she'd revealed but quick reflexes saved it from hitting the floor. "You want me to test out... an arm?"

She turned toward him and waved the arm between them. "I dunno. I hope you're not thinking that I need a toy."

Vincent saw the flash of humor in her eyes before she started to laugh.

Lily sat down in the chair and turned the arm over and over before her. "This feels almost real."

"That's the aim." Vincent grabbed the extra chair that he'd had delivered and pulled it closer before he sat down beside her. "It's a waste to buy pigs from butchers to use as practice canvases. No need to waste something people can eat."

He saw her nose wrinkle at the idea.

"I know it's the closest thing to human skin," she acknowledged, "but I'm not hating the idea that I won't have to do that to practice my skills."

He gave her a wink. "Exactly. You can use the practice arm to learn how to lay ink the right way. And there's quite a bit of surface area on it."

Lily turned the arm over again, tilting her head to the side to look at it along the surface. "It's also a good way to see that a design is laid out to flatter with its placement."

Vincent reached out his left hand and set it on her thigh. "You're so damn smart, Sweets."

"I'm a girl with limited income, Hotness."

He opened his mouth to argue with her, but she jumped in first.

"Don't you dare think that because I'm staying here with you right now that I'm going to let you pay for my training materials. I saved up for this."

"Yes," he gave her thigh a gentle squeeze, "you did, but Bill hasn't really made use of your time. The way I see it, Ink Envy owes you some supplies."

The look she gave him made his heart ache in his chest. She wasn't just beautiful, she was everything he never knew he wanted.

Seeing her in his shop that first day, he understood the whole concept of love at first sight.

He'd just been too stubborn and mulish to understand what... or rather, *who* was right there in front of him.

He wasn't going to waste any more time.

"And this thing about staying here *right now*?" He swept his thumb back and forth along the inside of her thigh. "Now that I have you here, I'm hoping to make it so good you want to stay."

She blushed all the way to the tips of her ears. "Well, so far you're doing a bang-up job of making me feel good again and again."

He loved that she could tease and still blush about it. "And I'll keep doing whatever I can to make you feel good."

She licked her lips and met his heated gaze with her own hungry look. "You take such good care of me, Vincent." Turning her chair toward his, she reached past his arm for his zipper. "I think I would like to take care of you, too."

Holy shit.

Vincent had always been seen as a hard ass in all the circles of his life.

Wouldn't it surprise folks if they found out that all it took was Lily touching the tip of her finger to the aching head of his cock to turn him into fucking silly putty? He'd never live it down.

"Shit, Sweets. That feels so good."

When she leaned over and kissed him he stopped caring who knew what as long as he got to keep this woman.

His woman.

— BIG 'N BURLY DUO 2 —

LILY

Later that night when Vincent was sound asleep in bed, she had moved back to their desk.

Their desk.

That's what he'd called it earlier.

He'd also been using the same word for a lot of things in the house.

Their bathroom.

Their kitchen.

And yes, *their* bedroom and *their* bed.

She had a feeling that if she told pretty much anyone how fast their relationship had progressed, those people would think she was crazy.

Well, those people also thought she was crazy to quit her jobs and be an unpaid drudge for an asshole artist just to learn how to be a tattoo artist herself.

And yet, here she was finally about to put ink into 'skin' and it wasn't her mentor who was making it possible.

It was Vincent.

It was so easy to love him that she was sure she was at least partially crazy.

Crazy like a fox.

She heard a soft groan and an exhale and she got up from the chair to look over the half-wall at the bed. The doctor had given him a brace to wear once the swelling had gone down and he should be okay sleeping with it on, but that didn't mean she wasn't worried.

Vincent groaned softly and reached out his left arm across her side of the bed. "Baby?"

Blinking back happy tears, Lily moved around to the bed on the other side of the room. "I'm here."

He propped himself up on his elbow and blinked into the half-light. "Everything okay?"

Lily crawled up onto the bed and over to his side. The thing was a California King and she felt like it would work as a raft in the middle of the ocean.

Kiss my ass, Rose.

She'd save her Jack on a raft this damn big.

Lily tucked her legs under as she leaned into his side looking down at his handsome face.

Lightly, she lifted her hands and smoothed her fingertips over his hair, his beard and his mustache and she couldn't help the soft sighs of wonder that escaped her lips. "I'm fine, Vincent. I'm still shocked at what you're doing to help me practice."

"You should have had the supplies already, but there's something else you should know."

"Oh? You love me, I know that already," she leaned down against his chest and combed her fingers through his beard, reveling in the sensation of his hair against her skin. "And I should tell you before you start to wonder, that besides crushing on you since before I even came into the shop, I love you like crazy."

He lifted up his good arm and slipped his fingers through her hair. He grabbed a fistful and brought her down to his lips for a kiss.

The way he all but devoured her mouth had her body singing and her nipples pressing into his chest in hard points.

When he let her up for air she could only stare at him in wonder.

Then when he spoke, she almost laughed. She'd forgotten that he was going to say something else.

"Those supplies that came in? Those are my prototypes. I'm ready to start my own supply company."

She shook her head and stared at him in wonder. "You are just incredible, you know that?"

He shook his head. "I want to help people get a start in this industry," he gazed longingly at her in the half-dark room. "And I'm hoping that in time I'll get to have some free time to take you on trips or maybe expand the house or-"

She kissed him.

Square on the mouth.

Wiggled her arm under his neck so that she could lean over him, nose to nose.

"Are you talking about a family?"

"You and me, Sweets. I could be happy with that if you didn't... if you don't want more."

Lily wiggled a little closer, relishing the friction of her body on his. And, if the hard line of his cock against her belly was anything to go by, he liked it too.

"There's something about you, Vincent Kane." She shifted over him, straddling his thighs. "It's habit forming, you know?"

His eyebrows lifted in reaction. "Me?"

"Yep." She licked her lips and nodded. "You."

"So..."

"So," she echoed his soft searching tone, "I'm in this, Vincent. You and me. Whatever else life gives us? I want that too."

He gave her a deep, sensuous kiss. "Good," he growled. "Now, let me hold you for a bit before we get up and get you working on that arm."

She snuggled down beside him. "Sounds good to me."

And it did.

It really did.

CHAPTER FOURTEEN

VINCENT

The day when his doctor fit him for a lightweight brace for his wrist and hand, Vincent felt as if a page had turned in the book of his life.

The swelling had gone down enough that he had increased function in his hand and fingers. He felt so much better, he just didn't want to risk his recovery.

And part of that was his relationship with Bill.

Not personally.

His business relationship.

He had to take real steps to end it if he wanted to move forward and spend his time doing what he wanted to do.

Build a new shop and be with Lily.

Both ideas were exciting, *really exciting* for him.

He took out his phone and looked through the contacts and found an old friend he could talk to. Angelique Monroe. He'd done some ink for her when he was starting out.

Before he hit the CALL button, he heard some movement in the hall.

"Hey," Lily leaned in through the open doorway and gave him a hesitant smile, "Ginger wants to make a run to Milk & Honey to get some snacks. Are you okay if I go with her?"

Perfect.

"Go. Have some fun with Ginger. Just make sure to bring me back something, too."

She pursed her lips together and gave him a shrug. "Maybe..."

"Maybe?"

Lily looked up at the ceiling before dropping her gaze back to him. "You know I will."

She moved into the room and he saw how gorgeous she looked. Since he'd seen her mostly in her work clothes, he didn't know what she liked to wear outside of the shop.

It turned out that while she wore a lot of black at the shop, she really liked colors and heaven help him, dresses that flowed over her body in ways that worked him up.

Lily noticed the look in his eyes.

Hell, she was responsible for the pain he'd be in, so she better notice.

"You sure you don't want me to stay here? I can go with Ginger for lunch another day or-"

"Go." He shook his head. "You're too damn tempting and I need to make a call or two. I'll be fine."

When she narrowed her eyes at him, he sighed.

"No heavy lifting. I promise."

She searched his gaze before she replied. "Okay. But know this: If I come back with some of Poppy's amazing baked goods and I even think you've jeopardized your recovery, I'm going to... I'm going to..."

Vincent sat back in his chair and shook his head, smiling.

"You're too damn adorable when you're all worked up, Sweets."

Her mouth gaped open for a moment until she closed it shut and gave him a half-serious glare. "I'm trying to be stern here."

"You're all kinds of stern, Lily. You're just all kinds of sweet and sexy too. Now go and get me some sugar."

She gave him a sour look but her eyes were full of light and humor. "You're walking a line, buster. Be good while I'm gone."

Less than a minute later he heard the front door close and lock.

"God, I love that woman."

He dialed the number he had for Angelique and waited while the call dialed through.

It picked up a few rings in.

"Vincent! How are you?"

"I'm good and not so good."

He heard a bunch of noise on the other end of the phone before it stopped.

"Sorry, I was walking through the court building and I ducked into the break room." He heard her soft sigh. "Finally, I get to sit. Is there something I can help with?"

"I'm that transparent, huh?" He felt a twinge in his neck, a sure sign that he was letting the stress get to him. "It has been a while since we talked."

"Well, if you recall, I did say you could call me anytime if there's something I can do for you."

"I thought it was the endorphins talking," he chuckled. "You sat like a rock for the six hours it took for your tattoo. By the end I thought you'd hit some sort of metaphysical high. I wasn't even sure if you'd remember what you said."

"No. Of course I remember, even if I was on a high back

then. It was exactly what I needed to celebrate passing the Bar Exam! And the tattoo still looks like gold! One of the paralegals in my office is totally jealous of how good my ink looks. I was going to send her your way."

"Well, that's the thing. I might not be at that shop for long."

"That shop? Hmm... What's going on?"

He opened his mouth to speak but she jumped back in.

"It's that guy, right? That asshole I keep seeing on social media surrounded by half-naked women. Bill something? He has that horrible nickname... Hannibal!"

"Exactly," he sighed. "I was wondering if you knew someone who deals in contract law."

"I know a bunch of folks for every kind of law, Vincent, but you're going to need someone who does contract and business law. Let me send a text to you with their contact information. You can't go wrong with Alex Layton. Crack law school student. She almost beat me to the top of the class. Almost."

"That's high praise from you."

She laughed. "I'm very competitive in school and in the courtroom, but I have to acknowledge how good she is. Otherwise, I wouldn't suggest that you see her. I hope this works out for you, Vincent.

"When you've started new somewhere else, call me. I'm in the mood to get another tattoo. I'm leaving private practice and going to work for the District Attorney's office."

"I'm impressed."

"Really? Most of my firm thinks I've lost my ever-lovin' mind."

"That depends on why you're doing it." He knew what she was going to say but he waited for her to answer.

"I want to help people get justice. And yes, I can do that from private practice, but I talked to the District Attorney at he last Bar Association meeting. I think you'd like her. She's tall and gorgeous and doesn't take shit from anyone. Let me know if you want to meet Valerie Wielding."

Vincent didn't have any interest at all. "I'm... I'm in love."

There.

He'd said it to someone else besides Lily.

The old grumpy gus that he'd been didn't even hurt a bit.

"Really? That's wonderful, Vincent! Now I really have to hurry you along to get your new shop open, because I'm betting there'll be pictures of her up on the walls."

"Well, she'll be an artist at the shop, so you'll see her."

Damn. He was so full of pride for Lily and how fast she was becoming a great tattoo artist. She had a real natural skill for putting ink in skin.

Hell, he was tempted to display her practice pieces on the website when he was ready to sell their products.

"So I'm going to let you go," she told him. "You need to call Alex and get to work. And I have to get back to my firm for an afternoon appointment. So, you take care, Vincent. I wish you only the best."

He managed to offer much the same and ended the call, but his focus was on Lily and the shop that they were going to build together.

He was a damn lucky man.

His phone pinged and he looked down at the screen. Angelique had sent him the contact information for Alex Layton.

He touched the screen and his phone dialed the number.

It was time to move on.

– BIG 'N BURLY DUO 2 –

LILY

Lily looked up from her work at the kitchen table. While drawing at Vincent's worktable was great with all of his lights, the kitchen table had amazing sunlight in the late afternoon and she was on a roll.

As wonderful as all of the styles were in tattooing, the style that she was developing a real affinity for was photorealism. Vincent's black and grey technique was amazing and she did love the clean lines of it and the shading that could be created on skin. Photorealism was closer to Ginger's style and so Lily could see that she'd be spending some serious hours at Ginger's shop observing her work.

Earlier, Ginger had stopped by to see Vincent and she took him over to the shop across from Milk & Honey to talk details about remodeling.

Both of them had encouraged Lily to go along, but she was really starting to get in the groove. She was working on a piece that she wanted to show Vincent later on. It wasn't a full piece, not in the traditional sense, but a focused piece of Vincent's eyes.

Smiling, Lily sat back and admired the intense gaze staring back at her.

It had started as a sketch in the wee hours of the morning a few days before.

She wasn't sure she could say it out loud, but it was a sketch of the first time that Vincent had gone down on her. The way his eyes watched her as she reached the precipice of arousal and fell right over the edge into that first amazing orgasm with his mouth on her.

She just couldn't forget the look in his eyes.

And now, she bit into her lower lip, she was trying to recreate that look in ink.

Lily knew she was getting close, but she wasn't quite ready to show it to him.

She certainly couldn't work on it with him awake. So when Ginger had stopped by, Lily had jumped at the chance to have the time alone.

For the first time in her life, Lily felt like she was finally on the right path. Finally, in the right place in her professional and personal life.

Shit, she shook her head. *I really shouldn't jinx this.*

Picking up her cell phone, she looked at the messages Vincent had sent a little while ago.

> VINCENT: Bringing dinner home. Hope you're hungry.
>
> VINCENT: This place is packed! I guess there's a reason why this place has so many good reviews.
>
> VINCENT: Still waiting. Going to need your help when we get back. Apparently, I ordered half the menu.

Good, she grinned, *I'm starving.*

She sat up like a shot when she heard a car door slam outside.

Was that...

Was this just crazy awesome timing?

Smiling, Lily felt a strange little shiver down her spine. Of course it was!

If there was something she'd learned over the last few weeks, it was that timing was just something she had to get used to.

She had been so used to things grinding along, but after

she'd ended up in the conflict with Bill and Vincent, her life had just starting chugging along like a train instead of the stationary bike she felt like she'd been on.

"Hey!"

She heard the voice outside and rushed to cover the rectangular tattoo base that Vincent's production company had mailed along with the other prototypes. It felt odd putting his eyes on a body part, even if it was fake.

With her work covered, she got up from the table and headed for the door to help Vincent with the take out bags.

The door slammed open and just missed her.

The man who walked through a moment later was Bill Baldwin.

And before he even said a word, she smelled the scent of cheap alcohol as if he'd bathed in it.

"Where the fuck are you, man?"

The sweet rush of anticipation at seeing Vincent turned into the cold hand of fear as Bill's watery eyes found her.

"You..."

She held up her hands in front of her. "Vincent..."

Her mind was racing. She could try to lie, but the house wasn't big enough that he would believe that Vincent was there but not coming out to see what the yelling was about.

"He's coming home right now, Bill. You should leave before he comes home."

"Comes. Home." Bill shook his head. "You've made yourself right at home, haven't you."

She swallowed. Hard.

"I was helping to take care of him after he hurt his hand."

"You mean after he clocked me to play white knight to your whiny ass."

"Please, Bill. Go before he comes home."

In hind sight, she'd realize what set him off, but in that moment she felt like he'd turned on a dime.

Bill stomped his foot on the hardwood floor and pointed at her face. He screamed at her with spittle flying from his lips. "You stupid little bitch!"

Lily turned her head to see the space around her.

There were doors that she could get behind, but they weren't close and Bill... Well, Bill was tall and had the legs that went with that height.

"Bill, stop."

"*Bill, stop.*" He mimicked her voice in a high squeak and then let loose with a curse. "You wouldn't say that if you were fucking me."

Lily's skin was cold.

Clammy.

She felt like she'd stepped into a deep freezer and the temperature kept dropping.

"Bill, please."

She took a few steps back hoping that he wouldn't see where she was headed.

"That's better, bitch." He lifted his hand from his side and that's when she saw the bottle of alcohol in his hand. "Want a drink to take the edge off?"

He wiggled the bottle and she heard the liquor sloshing around inside of it. A few drops even made it up through the neck and out onto his hand.

"Come on, baby. Take a drink. Maybe I'll bend you over that table and see what you're offering." He took a step forward and she turned to run.

That's when the socks she was wearing tripped her up, sending her crashing down to the floor.

Lily saw the floor rushing up to her face and even though

she put her hands out to stop herself the impact drove her head into the ground.

She was stunned and her head rang, but she was clear enough to know what was happening to her when Bill picked her up off of the floor by the back of her shirt and shorts.

"Fucking bitch."

She put her hands out, but there was nothing to grasp. Nothing to get a hold of.

"Oof."

Whatever air she had in her lungs rushed out as he let her go.

The cool wood that her cheek landed on was the kitchen table.

Panic seized her.

She took a steadying breath and decided to reach for the tattoo machine that was in the center of the table. Maybe she could use it.

Lily dragged in a breath and started to move.

"Ah!"

Bill caught her hand an inch away from the machine and pulled it back behind her, pinning it there.

It was painful, but she was almost glad for that.

Pain fought the ache in her head. Kept her focused.

But panic really set in when she felt him against her back and the haze of alcohol in her face.

"I'm your mentor, remember? You're supposed to do what I want."

"Talk to me," she begged. "Why were you looking for Vincent? It wasn't because of me, was it?"

"It's all because of you, you little bitch."

The scent of alcohol from his breath was so strong she felt the bile spill onto the back of her tongue.

"Don't... don't do this, Bill. I haven't... I haven't done anything to you."

"Oh, yeah?" He slammed the bottle of liquor on the table just shy of her face. "It's because of you that I just got a bunch of papers from my lawyer saying that I'm losing my partner! I'm going to lose my whole fucking business because of a piece of ass!"

Move!

The voice in her head screamed at her.

Move, Lily!

She wriggled under him, her eyes shut, trying to feel just where he was.

He was too drunk to notice, but he was man enough to enjoy the friction.

That's when she went limp on the table and brought her leg up between his.

Bill howled at the sudden smack and let her hand go. Lily lifted her hand and reached for the tattoo machine.

She got her fingers around the power cord and yanked it closer just as her head cracked against the tabletop.

CHAPTER FIFTEEN

VINCENT

When Ginger's SUV turned onto their private road, Vincent saw the truck parked on the path to his front door.

Even at that distance, he knew whose truck it was. Painted along the side of the body were the words: HANNIBAL - TATTOO GOD.

He didn't even have to ask Ginger to speed up. She stomped on the gas pedal, and they rocketed forward.

And before she'd even come to a complete stop, Vincent was out of the truck, the bags full of food spilling out behind him onto the ground.

As he pounded up the walkway, he and Ginger shouted over each other.

"Call the police!"

"I'm calling the police!"

. . .

The front door was hanging open, but that didn't matter. Vincent would have gone through the door if he had to.

He wasn't going to let Bill hurt Lily. Vincent's only thought was getting her to safety.

Vincent came to an abrupt stop just inside the door, and his heart almost stopped as well.

"Look who came to dinner!"

Bill had Vincent's life in his hands.

Or rather, he had it pinned to the dining table.

Lily wasn't moving and her eyes weren't open. Vincent could only hope that she was unconscious.

He didn't want her to have any memories of what was happening.

"Let her go, Bill."

His soon to be ex partner looked shocked.

"You want me to let her go?" His laugh was odd, high-pitched and almost manic. "If I do, she's going to hit the floor. She doesn't exactly have control of her body."

"Set her down gently."

Bill just stared at him. "I don't see where you have any control here, asshole. You're the one who started this ball rolling. I'm just trying to make this shit show entertaining."

"There's nothing entertaining about what's going on." Vincent ground his words through his clenched teeth. "And if you want to hurt someone. I'm right here."

Vincent moved in closer, trying to move toward the side of the table closest to Lily, but hoping that Bill would keep his focus on him.

Ego was a strong motivator for Bill.

"You don't want to hurt her, Bill. Not really."

"Oh? I suppose you're going to tell me why?"

"Yeah." Vincent gave him a short nod. "I already had those papers drawn up before she ever came into the shop."

Vincent had been told time and time again that when he narrowed his eyes, he looked like a hard ass. It had never been intentional.

Until now.

"You're a mess, Bill. You're a complete jackass, too. I've been trying to find a way to shake you loose and then you gave me the ammunition I needed to pull the trigger, legally."

Bill's expression soured as if he smelled something vile and he shook his head like he was trying to clear it.

"Your client, Bambi?"

Bill's upper lip twisted in a sneer. "Bitch threw me out the day after I got there."

"Yeah, I know." He saw Bill's jaw dropped down, but before he could say anything, Vincent pushed on. "She got a hold of your phone while you were bent over her toilet, emptying your stomach. She found the text messages you sent some of your other clients."

Bill shook his head and shrugged his shoulders, unable to see what damage he'd done to himself.

"And found some text message you'd sent to another tattoo artist looking to sell your interest in Ink Envy for some quick cash."

A dark cloud settled over Bill's features as his words settled in.

"Nah, Vin. That's shit. She didn't see anything like that. She's makin' up stories."

Vincent had moved another step closer, but Bill seemed focused on the way his life was imploding.

"I've got the screenshots that she took of your phone and the messages you wrote. I bet you didn't read the whole filing that my lawyer sent to you."

Bill shrugged, a quick twitch of his shoulders. "So what? You're ending our partnership. What the fuck difference would it be to read the whole damn thing?"

"Yeah, I didn't think you'd read our original partnership papers either. You broke one of the clauses in our agreement that was the first right of refusal when one of us wanted out. You were required to offer me the chance to buy you out."

Maybe it was the booze, or maybe Bill was finally thinking clearly for the first time in a long time.

"I don't..." He staggered a little, his brow furrowing above his nose. "What the—"

Vincent rushed the table and pushed in between Bill and Lily, wrapping his arms around her.

Bill stumbled and hit the ground with a sickening crack, but Vincent didn't care to look and see what the man had fallen on.

Holding Lily, Vincent fell to his knees, cradling her against his chest.

"Lily?"

There were other voices in the room then. Shouting. Boots pounding on the floor.

None of it mattered.

Vincent tilted her head back so he could look at her face.

She looked like she was sleeping, and he leaned in with his cheek against her nose. The soft puff of her breath kept him sane.

"Vincent?"

He heard Ginger's voice, but it sounded like she was miles away.

"Come on, baby." He rubbed at Lily's arm, trying to rouse her. Continuing as she lay silent and unmoving in his arms. "Look at me."

"Vincent?"

He felt Ginger's hand on his shoulder and barely managed not to shrug it off.

She was trying to help.

To support him and Lily, but he didn't want anyone touching him besides Lily.

He was so far gone over his woman.

"The EMTs are pulling up outside."

He didn't wait for them to come in or even up to the front door.

Vincent got up on his feet with Lily held against his chest and met them out on the path.

He laid her on the gurney and walked beside it to the ambulance, his gaze unerringly on her face.

"I'm right here, Sweets. I'm right here."

That's when he saw her eyes open again, her hand reaching for his.

"Thank fuck." He shook his head and lifted her hand to his mouth to brush a kiss across her knuckles. "It's so good to see your pretty, pretty eyes."

She managed a soft smile of her own. "It's good to see you to."

CHAPTER SIXTEEN

LILY

It was a few weeks before Lily managed to talk Vincent into inking her. The frustrating man had treated her like fine bone China since that evening at the house.

Bill's upcoming trial was weighing heavily on Vincent and it seemed that every time that they came close to shutting the door on that horrible memory, Vincent would tense up and take a trip to the new shop across the way from Milk & Honey.

It was just such a trip that Lily used to break through the problem.

The whole thing took some doing and help from a number of their friends.

Ginger was the one who intercepted him before he managed to get down the long private drive.

A feigned problem with her wireless router got Vincent in her home and gave Lily a chance to sneak into town.

Ronan was there to open the doors and let Lily into the shop to set up her surprise and Poppy was right there too, helping to keep Lily's nerves in check.

It helped Lily focus on the future that Poppy had already put dibs on Lily's first client session and the two of them talked about the design for Poppy's tattoo while they set up the inks and Vincent's tattoo machine.

By the time Vincent finally arrived at 'Kiss of Ink', he had no idea what was going on.

And when he opened the door to his personal studio he saw Lily waiting for him on the brand new ink chair.

Lily recognized the exact moment when her handsome man went from shock to hunger.

It was the look in his eyes.

The same look that she had captured in her practice tattoo work.

The look that she'd shown him the night before, completed.

"What are doing, Sweets?"

Oh, she did love the rough tone of his voice as he approached the chair.

He hesitated when he saw the design that she'd transferred onto her skin.

"Lily-love. Are you sure?"

She nodded and he reached out to trace the long stem of one of the flowers in the design.

"It's the design you drew while I was going through tests at the Emergency Room. The design that I found when I woke up and you were asleep on the edge of my bed. Pink Lily of the Valley. You remember what you told me?"

He nodded and pulled his chair over to the side of the tattoo chair. "True love and femininity. Admiration."

She smiled and put her hand over his.

"I was so afraid that something would change between us after Bill broke into the house. Like you would decide that what we had... had been ruined somehow.

"And maybe it was the headache talking. Goodness knows it hurt like crazy, but I was so worried that you'd think I was too much trouble or worry."

He turned his hand so that he could weave their fingers together. "I would never have forgiven myself if you'd been permanently injured by him. I beat myself for leaving you alone and-"

"The decision to stay home was mine."

"But I should have told you about the papers my lawyer sent him."

She listened to the words and shrugged. Finally, he'd said the words to her. He'd been silent and withdrawn at times, worrying her.

Now she knew what he'd been holding inside.

The thoughts that had been swirling in his head.

He'd been torturing himself for nothing.

"Whether or not you told me didn't dictate what Bill did. He was drunk. He was angry. And you can't tell me that Bill doesn't get drunk and angry all the time on his own. Can you?"

Vincent looked up into her eyes and she saw the anguish in his expression. "But he took it out on you."

"He's the only one responsible for his actions. And you're responsible for yours."

He narrowed his eyes at her, probably searching for her meaning.

So she gave it to him.

"Your gift to me that night in the hospital. When I woke up with you at my side. Your amazing artwork and the meaning behind it?

"That's what I held onto and knew that everything was going to be okay."

Vincent shook his head and she saw him blink back tears. "Baby, you amaze me."

Smiling, she gave his hand a squeeze. "You give me life, Vincent Kane. Now, I want you to give me my first ink. A Vincent Kane original."

He was chuckling with laughter moments later, and she let out a sigh of relief.

"You want me to ink you."

She licked her lips and smiled. "I *need* you to ink me."

He sighed loudly and reached for the box of gloves on the rolling supply tray in arm's reach. "Fuck me."

"Well, I've been trying," she settled into the tattoo chair, and gave him a broad smile, "I've certainly been trying."

Two weeks later, Lily was chomping at the bit to get the thumbs up from Vincent.

He'd taken her ink aftercare to an extreme, in her opinion.

Ginger wasn't much help, laughing every time they saw each other and sadly siding with Vincent.

Or rather siding with him that it was up to the artist to decide when it had healed up enough to withstand a bit of… stress.

But Lily was done.

Quite done, in fact.

She was ready to tie him down if she needed to and get on with her life.

So while he was at court, finalizing the dissolution of his partnership with Bill, Lily was at home waiting.

And this time, when she heard the door slam outside, she knew who it was because she'd been tracking Vincent's phone.

It was an app they started using to ease both of their minds after Bill had broken the door.

She heard Vincent's tread up the steps to the porch and she smiled when he tried to put the key in the lock.

The door swung open at the touch of the key against the lock and he lifted his head to look inside the house.

That's when she gave him a brilliant smile. "Welcome home, sweetheart. You look like you're ready for bed."

"Bed, huh?" He looked down at his suit and tie. "I look like I'm ready for the office."

She put her hands on her lower back which pulled the silk of her negligee tight across her breasts. "I'm okay with doing it in your office. It'll be another memory on that amazing table of yours."

Lily heard a rumble in his chest and then the heavy thump of his briefcase on the floor.

"I'm a weak man, Sweets."

She crooked her finger at him and he locked the door before he walked across the room to stand in front of her.

"You're the strongest man I know, Vincent Kane."

He shook his head. "Hardly. My cousin Amos? He's a Federal Marshal. I'm a-"

"You're caring. Talented. Sinfully so. And you're sexy."

"Sexy, huh?"

She knew that he was playing. Encouraging her.

"Super sexy." She put her hands on his chest and leaned up to kiss the corner of his mouth. "Fucking sexy."

"Fucking?"

She heard his voice growl in his throat and she smiled like a kitty cat. Sneaky and satisfied.

"I said what I said, big man." She drew her hands down his chest and let her fingertips trail over his belly and down even further. "Now, let's get these pants off of you."

"F...."

She slipped her hand in through the open zipper of his pants.

"...uck."

"That's what I'm trying to do, Vincent." She bit into her lip as his dick twitched in her hand. "See? You want to, too."

He reached his arms around her and grabbed her ass, pulling her tight against his chest.

She was breathless at the way the silk of her gown tugged at her tightened nipples.

"Maybe," he sucked in a breath, "I should take a look at your tattoo first."

She tipped her head back and stared at the ceiling. "Vincent! Enough! Just-"

His lips touched her throat and opened in a hot kiss against her skin.

The slight scratch of his beard against her skin made her skin tingle all over her body.

When his lips reached her collarbone, she knew she was gone, a complete mess.

"Vincent, god..."

She felt him smile against her shoulder and her knees buckled.

"Whoa, careful now."

Before she could wrap her mind around what was happening, Vincent bent down and put her over his shoulder.

She was laughing when he carried her into their bedroom, one arm around her back, the other on her backside.

– BIG 'N BURLY DUO 2 –

VINCENT

"I love you like my next breath." He looked down at her laid out on their bed.

Her silk gown was hiked up to the tops of her thighs and her hands pulled the thin straps down over her shoulders.

"Damn it, Lil. You look like a fucking wet dream."

His beautiful woman smoothed a hand over her breasts and down between her thighs. She lifted the hem with one hand and slipped two fingers from her other hand between her legs.

When she drew it out again, she turned her hand around to show him.

He saw her fingers glistening with her arousal.

"Fuck me." He'd already ditched his coat, so he tugged his shirt open in a way that tore a couple of buttons from the fabric. He dropped his pants down a second later and got up onto the mattress as fast as he could.

Lily tried to pull away, laughing, but he grasped her wrist and held her hand still as he sucked her fingers into his mouth.

"Yes," she sighed, "tongue. I want to feel your.... yes."

Just hearing her voice and her breathy sighs had his dick swelling, near to bursting with need.

His gorgeous girl.

His sweet, sweet love.

He twisted her wrist slightly and sucked her fingers deeper into his mouth.

She tasted so damn sweet, like honey, fresh and warm on his tongue and-

He heard her laughter while her other hand slid up and down his dick.

"Oh," she laughed, a throaty, sexy sound, "he likes that."

He pulled her fingers from his mouth with a soft pop.

"*He* doesn't like it, babe. He fucking loves it."

Letting go of her wrist entirely, he reached for her, lifting the hem of her gown until it was up above her hips.

He was turning into a sentimental fool.

Vincent almost wept at the sight of his ink on her belly. Placed in the curve of her hipbone, the bouquet of flowers he'd inked on her looked as though he'd laid lily of the valley stems against her skin just moments before.

Vincent traced his fingers down over the stems almost reverently.

"I love you, Lily."

Her movements made the slightest sound against their sheets and he looked up to see her tug the neckline of it down, exposing her breasts to his hungry eyes.

"I love you too, Vincent."

Fuck. He felt his dick twitch as his balls swelled and ached for release.

He'd been dreaming of making love with Lily for... much too long.

Vincent shook his head. "I want to make this last, but-"

"I feel like I'm about to explode, Vincent."

Wiggling lower on the bed, Lily drew her legs up before dropping her knees to the sheets.

She was wide open before him, her eyes hazy with need. "Worry about lasting later, hmm? I need to feel you inside me, Vincent."

He felt her need.

Fuck, he felt the same way, like he'd lose his damn mind if he didn't bury himself-

"Yes... oh god, yes!"

Vincent looked down and shook his head to clear his thoughts.

He was inside her.

And he'd never felt anything like it before.

She was wet and hot and the way her body grasped at his cock made him feel like he might just stay like that forever.

He felt her muscles stroke him, squeeze him, pull him deeper.

It was hard to believe that this beautiful woman wanted him. He wasn't muscle bound or a model of any kind. He spent most of his time hunched over, drawing or putting ink into skin, but here she was looking at him as if he was everything to her.

Good. She was everything to him.

"Vincent?"

He looked up into her gorgeous eyes.

"Did I lose you?"

She smiled at him with a spark of humor mixed in with the desire in her eyes.

"Lost in your head?"

Lily was truly made for him.

He grasped her hips and shook his head as he pulled her harder onto his cock.

Her lips parted in a breathy sigh.

"I'm lost in you, Lily."

And he proceeded to show her how much.

HIDDEN BY THE DAD BOD

Amos & April find themselves literally thrown together at the beginning of a wild winter storm and find shelter in each other.

Amos Kane

He was forced to retire early as a U.S. Marshal when he lost a witness and nearly his life. Since that time, he's been happy, well 'relatively' happy to hunker down in the woods by his lonesome.

No one needs to deal with his anger and disappointment.

A WITSEC marshal shows up and leaves a witness on his doorstep before speeding off to catch a suspect.

He wasn't even given the chance to say no and try as hard as he can to keep his distance he finds himself drawn to her. Damn it.

April Reynolds

April's life was simple and easy until that morning. A stop at a roadside fruit stand ends when she's a witness to a double murder.

Being out in the middle of nowhere she's surprised when

a federal agent takes her into the woods and drops her off at a cabin owned by the grumpiest man she'd ever seen.

Too bad he was also the most attractive man she'd ever met. Shoot and double shoot.

April isn't used to hiding away from the world. She likes meeting people and spending time with them, but the cabin tucked away in the woods and its own have their own charm. She's just not sure things will work out Hidden by the Dad Bod

ABOUT REINA TORRES

Reina reads like she writes-
- Heat to Sweet
- Contemporary to Historical
- Normal to Paranormal
- Military,
- First Responders
- & More
- Always with an HEA because we all deserve the same!

Made in the USA
Columbia, SC
15 June 2024